"A CLASSIC SEA CHASE."
—*St. Louis Post Dispatch*

EVERY DECISION NERGER MADE NOW
WAS MADE WITH ONE END IN VIEW: TO
INFLICT MAXIMUM DAMAGE ON THE
ENEMY, WITH MINIMUM DANGER TO HIS
SHIP AND CREW. THIS WAS WARTIME—
AND THIS WAS THE WAY IT HAD TO
BE . . .

RAIDER WOLF

WOLF

THE VOYAGE OF
CAPTAIN NERGER, 1916-1918

by Edwin P. Hoyt

PINNACLE BOOKS   NEW YORK CITY

This is a work of fiction. All the characters and events portrayed in this book are fictional, and any resemblance to real people or incidents is purely coincidental.

RAIDER WOLF

Copyright © 1974 by Edwin P. Hoyt

A Pinnacle Books edition, published by special arrangement with Paul S. Eriksson, Inc.

ISBN: 0-523-40005-X

First printing, February 1977

Published in Great Britain in 1974 by Arthur Barker Limited

Printed in the United States of America

PINNACLE BOOKS, INC.
275 Madison Avenue
New York, N. Y. 10016

Contents

1	The Ship	1
2	The Breakout	15
3	South to Africa—and Beyond	25
4	The Lonely Life of the Corsair	37
5	Time Is the Enemy	51
6	Sunday Island	63
7	None but the Enemy	77
8	The Third Phase	93
9	On the Attack	109
10	The Raider's Teeth	123
11	The Hunter Hunted	149
12	Heading Home	163
13	Northward Ho!	173
14	The Blockade	183
15	Breakthrough	193
16	Home Again	201
	Notes	209

RAIDER WOLF

1

The Ship

Fregattenkapitän Karl August Nerger paced the bridge nervously this spring morning, cigar clenched in teeth, and occasionally paused to scowl down into the swirling greasy waters of Hamburg harbour. His mind was awhirl with conflicting emotions.

Nerger, a mere leutnant-commander in the Imperial German Navy, had just been handed a task that could bring a bitter end to his hard-won naval career; or the challenge might offer him a hero's death at sea, and if he had the luck of heroes it might even bring him glory and the coveted *Pour le Mérite*, the highest decoration the Kaiser could bestow on one of his faithful servants. Round him, under him, lay reminders of the chances. A few days before Korvettenkapitän Nikolaus zu Dohna-Schlodien had steamed triumphantly into Heligoland Bight after a victorious cruise in the Raider *Möwe* that had cost Britain and Germany's other enemies some fifteen ships. Dohna-Schlodien's remarkable achievement had come at just the proper moment to revive sagging German morale. Back in the hot summer of 1914 the war had seemed glorious, but by the end of 1915 Kaiser Wilhelm's armies were mired in the mud before Verdun, digging trenches, launching bloody attacks that brought a few feet of territory at the awful cost of thousands of dead and wounded, and virtually getting nowhere. The navy had fared a little better, but not much. Early in the war the exploits of the German cruisers had warmed hearts at home. Karl von Müller in the *Emden* had set all the world a-talking about German naval brilliance, dash and courtliness, with a short but fruitful raiding cruise in the Indian Ocean. *Königsberg* had made her foray off the African coast, and now, bottled up in the river Rufiji, was still fighting gamely for life and tying up vast segments of the British navy. Admiral von Spee with his East Asia Squadron had whipped the British at Coronel, and then fallen prey to superior force in the Battle of the Falkland Islands, going down to a watery grave. These men were the heroes of the war: the admirals in Europe and the captains of the dreadnoughts had been thoroughly eclipsed. The German high seas fleet made a single dash into open water to engage enemy ships. The results of this Battle of Jutland would do little more than provide meat for naval historians, and bottle up the high seas fleet to a war of anxious frustration. By 1916 it was certain that raiding was where the action was going to be.

However, commerce raiding, of the kind conducted by von Müller and Dohna-Schlodien, had its pitfalls. Take *Greif*. The emperor himself had come down to Kiel to make a formal farewell and say "God speed" to Fregattenkapitän Tiesze and his men; they had sailed out bravely and hopefully, met the British auxiliary cruiser *Alcantara* and sunk her with a torpedo, and then been set upon themselves by a pair of British cruisers, to go down to that hero's death before even leaving the waters of the North Sea. That was a price that must be considered. Far worse was the fate that had befallen the ship on which Nerger now stood, her captain disgraced, the crew out of countenance, the mission unfulfilled. The crewmen called her *Wolf*, for that was the name they had taken back in 1915 when the liner *Belgravia* had been put into commission as a raider. She had been almost ready to steam out on the day that *Greif* left, but not quite. Grand precautions had been taken to mislead English spies, *Belgravia* had been fitted with a false funnel and all sorts of wild rumours had infiltrated the shipyards. But then on the eve of departure there had been an accident in the engine-room, the half-trained firemen had panicked, deserting the engine-room chief in the escaping steam. The boiler had exploded, *Belgravia* had begun taking water and had been unceremoniously towed back to the naval base by tugboats, the voyage aborted, the captain's career destroyed.

These were the dangers and the opportunities, and as the slender, middle-sized Captain Nerger paced his useless deck he knew them full well. The thing now, this spring morning, was to find a new ship, get her fitted out and get to sea. The name *Wolf* had a sour ring to it at headquarters, and yet such were the traditions and stiffness of the service that no one thought of changing the raider's name after the bad experience. The mission would be the same, and all was coded together. Nerger was the new captain of the *Wolf*; he simply had to find a ship to bear the name. Donning his long frock-coat with the four stripes of his rank, putting the braided cap squarely on his head the way he wore it, Nerger set his narrow face in determination and began to prowl the cluttered wharves of Hamburg harbour, looking for a ship.

At one berth was the banana transport *Ulan*, a relic of happy pre-war days when Germany's major effort at sea had been an attempt to capture foreign markets from the envied English. She was the sister ship of *Möwe*. Would she not serve Nerger's purpose marvellously? He looked her over with the delight of a seafaring man over a handsome ship; she was modern, rakish, roomy and fast. Fast—yes that was the trouble. She was too fast, she ate up coal like a racehorse going through the oat bin; she had everything a captain could want in a raider but she could not be used. Nerger's mission was to sail half-way round the world to the Indian Ocean, and he wanted to get there. He knew from the record of von Müller and Dohna-Schlodien and the rest that his major problem would be supply. The *verdammt* British had bases all over the seven seas; now, in 1916, Germany had none. All her colonies had been cap-

tured or were under siege and useless. Nerger
would have to rely on captures, on his own inge-
nuity and courage. Speed in a ship was lovely, but
stealth was what was wanted. Reluctantly, Nerger
passed beautiful *Ulan* by, and went on.

He dismissed half a dozen other ships—fast, too
small, hoggish, water-weary. It was too bad about
Belgravia, he mused, for she would have been ad-
mirable. Built in a British yard, she carried the
unmistakable finish of an Englishman; she, too,
had been a part of Germany's effort to capture su-
zerainty over the sea lanes in those peaceful days.
Germany had no experience in building liners, so
the Hamburg-Amerika line had gone abroad to get
the best. But that was all behind. *Belgravia* could
not be got ready for a year, and Nerger was not
really sorry. For she, too, was a coal-burning racehorse of the sea. The captain brushed off the past,
and looked squarely to the future, marching along
the quay, looking, looking. He found what he
must have that day. She was the Hansa line's
freighter *Wachtfels*. She was big, squat and
sturdy; employed on the Asiatic run. She would
have to do. Nerger did not even go aboard, but
turned on his heel and headed back for his cabin
on the ill-fated *Belgravia*.

Once there, he sent for the gunnery officer,
Leutnant-zur-See Witschetzky. This young man
was an expert, a transfer from the big ship
Prinzregent Luitpold, Admiral Funke's flagship of
the modern, powerful Third Squadron. Witschetzky knew his job and he would have to make
the final decision. Nerger waited. The younger
man arrived, opened the door, stepped in, saluted
and clicked his heels and stood straight at atten-

tion. The captain waved him into an easier pose, and then outlined the matter at hand. Witschetzky was to board the *Wachtfels*. He was to go alone and to say nothing to his brother officers. Only one thing was important: would the ship carry the weight and bear the recoil of seven 5.9 inch guns? Witschetzky was to find out, and then come back and report to the captain.

Witschetzky saluted again, spun around and out of the cabin, and headed for the wharves. Halfway down the harbour he found her, the iron cross of the Hansa line on her smokestack, surely a German-built ship, with her practical simple lines. The captain of the freighter was aboard, and Witschetzky could sense that he knew the young man's mission. The captain was cordial, but he left his cabin to show the officer around, and as they walked, the old man pointed out all the defects that *Wachtfels* would have as a naval vessel.

"I suppose you're thinking of making another *Möwe* of her," he said gloomily. "She would never do."

Witschetzky stepped gingerly over that verbal hurdle, embarrassed because he was in no position to discuss the matter at all, and they walked in silence.

"See what I mean," said the old man. "Here are the lascars' quarters. You certainly couldn't put a gun in here. There's no room for it."

The young officer was silent, but his eyes roamed the compartment. Knock out those bunks, tear away the false wooden bulkhead, and two 5.9 inch guns would go very nicely. Two more would go up on the forecastle.

They moved back up to the bridge and then to

the officers' quarters. Witschetzky moved around, estimating, looking this way and that. Two more guns would go here. He stopped and made a note. The captain watched, unhappily.

"It's a raw day," said the old man. "You're going to catch cold wandering around in this weather without a duffel coat. Come on below and we'll have a grog to warm you up."

The young officer smiled, but moved toward the stern. There, on the fantail, there was the place for that seventh gun. Captain Nerger had his new *Wolf*—no question about it. Witschetzky snapped shut his notebook, smiled at the captain, and they hastened below for a drink. After one or two, the old captain began to talk about the ship. He had taken her to the Indies twice and she was a good stout merchantman. But of course she would never make a warship of any kind. She could only make eleven knots with the safety valve tied down tight; she was only 5,600 tons—no size at all for a warship, as anyone could see. She couldn't possibly mount a gun or stand the recoil if a place could be found for one. The old man babbled on: the thing to do was send him out again to neutral ports to bring home supplies for the war, not send poor *Wachtfels* out alone to be a warrior.

A little steamy from the grog and the warmth of the cabin, Leutnant Witschetzky broke off the party and headed unsteadily back through the cold sharp air to his ship. By the time he reached Nerger's cabin he was in control again, and he made his report. Nerger puffed on his cigar and listened. Then he dismissed the leutnant. It was not a German captain's way to tell his subordinates what he was going to do. But soon enough

Witschetzky and the other men of *Wolf* learned that the admiralty had bought the *Wachtfels* from the Hansa line. The orders came: the crew was to move to the new ship and make her ready for sea. There would be no slip-up this time, Nerger made sure of that. Day and night he was on the ship, everywhere, from the forepeak to the bunker room, prowling, planning, giving instructions and supervising changes. When all was done that could be done at Hamburg, the crew got ready for sea, but a very short run, only to Wilhelmshaven, the big naval base, where the guns and munitions would be taken aboard and the *Wolf* would be given her teeth.

Nerger agreed with Leutnant Witschetzky's findings. The guns were installed as the younger officer had suggested, hidden from the workaday world by false bulkheads that swung away to reveal the weapons in all their ferocity. Four torpedo tubes were also added to the ship, so were a device for making artificial smoke (a good cover for a getaway) and mine-laying equipment. Whatever *Wolf* would be, she would never again be the innocent merchantman of the Indies trade.

There was no waste of effort or of space. The work went on during daylight hours under the hot summer sun. It went on at night under the bright lights of the dockyard. The crew worked sea watches to help the civilian mechanics who were fitting out their new home. It would not be a luxurious home—Fregattenkapitän Nerger had come up through the ranks of a harsh service which gave little thought to the creature comforts of the men below decks. The washrooms and lines of hammocks were to be brothers to the mines; every

8

inch of storage was used. It seemed odd, because whole compartments were set aside with bunks and tables, and the crew jammed up in the mine stowage. Nerger was looking ahead to the day when he would be at sea, sinking ships of the enemy and taking prisoners. *Wolf*, unlike most of her sister raiders, would be able to handle the unhappy passengers. Nerger had learned from the problems of Dohna-Schlodien and the others that some provision must be made for the captures. One of the great dangers faced by a commerce raider came with the return to port of a lifeboat crew of a sunken ship. The alarm would sound throughout the British Empire, all the naval forces in the area would congregate and begin to pinpoint the position of the raider, and unless she were very wary, and very lucky, eventually the ring would close on her. Nerger's idea was to destroy the evidence. It was a day of compassion at sea—he would not sink the enemy merchant ships and let the crews and passengers go down to Davy Jones (as his *confrères* in the submarine service were doing), but still he would preserve the essential element of secrecy and surprise by taking aboard *Wolf* the men of his victim ships.

Indeed, secrecy was the order of the day. Nerger and German intelligence now knew that *Greif* had gone to her death at least partially because British intelligence knew all about her before she ever sailed from the waters of the River Jade. There were spies even inside the sacred precincts of the naval base. So the name *Wolf* was never mentioned; the ship bore on her stern plates the pseudonym *Jupiter*, and never flew the German naval battle flag. She lay quietly, Nerger trying his best

9

to be inconspicuous, which was difficult that summer as the battered survivors of Jutland streamed into harbour, the battle cruiser *Derfflinger* to tie up alongside *Wolf*, her bridge askew, half shot off by British shells, her dead and wounded pouring ashore before the eyes of *Wolf*'s anxious and impatient crew.

Wolf seemed insignificant there. The Kaiser came and spoke brave words about the grand victory off the Skagerrack, and gave Admiral Scheer a medal amidst the huzzas of the fleet; there was much noisy shouting, singing and drinking around the taverns outside the base that night. Meanwhile, *Wolf* loaded, and loaded, and loaded. The old cargo holds were filled with coal, four times more than anyone thought she could handle. Nerger took her out of port from time to time, to conduct exercises with the crew, to train them to handle the guns and the torpedoes and to lay the mines. Always they went out quietly, no flags flying, the guns hidden behind their false fronts, half the crew warned sternly to remain below decks; for it was essential that *Wolf* play the part of a lonely merchantman when she finally began her mission at sea. The training exercises were long and wearying, conducted day and night, with Nerger roaming the ship and pacing the bridge, cigar in teeth. If a man stepped out of line, or made a foolish error, and the captain saw him, the poor man could expect a dressing down unrivalled by the toughest bosun in any navy's service. Somewhere Nerger had acquired a command of profanity so profound as to shock even a stevedore, and when a man erred, the captain would unleash the power of his invective with the speed of a cobra.

One of those tongue lashings kept a crewman on his toes for a week.

Gun Number Seven, the after gun, posed a bit of a problem, for to be effective the gun had to be placed right aft. How could that tell-tale snout be concealed? Nerger considered the matter, and consulted with the armaments officer of the base. He brought a little plan. Soon workmen were on the ship, putting up a "cargo boom." This was Number Seven. To be sure that it was well-camouflaged, the dockyard added two other, real, cargo booms. They were stationary; only the gun came down, to point toward the horizon, but from a distance of a few feet the difference was unrecognizable.

Nerger had left no idea untried. He knew that concealment was his finest weapon of defence, so the smokestack of *Wolf* was fixed to be unfixed— made convertible. It could be long and narrow. It could be short and squat. The masts telescoped, like the legs of a photographer's tripod. Below he had plans of many ships and the wherewithal in the paint locker and the carpenter's stores to adopt their lines and colours.

At one point, during the loading, it appeared that all Nerger's careful planning would be for nothing. One night, as the weary crew was at rest, came the shout from the lookouts:

"Fire. Fire in the after hold."

The alarms sounded, the bells clanged, the port awakened and men came rushing from all angles to save the ship. Those who knew blenched a little, for the fire in the coal hold had broken out just a few feet from the bulkhead that protected the ammunition. Nerger was up in an instant, directing the salvage effort.

"Get the ammunition out of there," he shouted to his second in command, Leutnant Brandes. Brandes sent damage control parties to move the shells and mines, and the rest of the crew was hustled into the steaming, smoking coal holds, with water playing onto the fire, to get the coal out.

Nerger was stunned. He was as restless as any man aboard the ship, and he had hoped to get away in the late summer or early fall. Now came a three week delay, while the ship was cleared and cleaned, the ammunition brought back behind reinforced bulkheads, and the coal reloaded. Now he wondered if he would ever get away. Three weeks fighting a stupid coal fire; more weeks getting off the remaining four thousand tons, now a sodden useless mass. The three hundred members of the crew were nearly exhausted at the end of it; certainly the augury was not good. Still, he perservered and no man of the crew ever knew how close he came to despair in the blackest moments. The clean-up was finished, more precious Ruhr coal was embarked, and the training exercises were redoubled.

Usually the *Wolf* steamed out into the Baltic for four or five days, then came in again. But one fall day, Nerger took them out for a week of intensive manoeuvres, and when the weekend came, the men were tired, and ready to meet their girls ashore and relax in the *Bierstuben* and *Weingärten* of Kiel's suburbs.

But this weekend, Captain Nerger showed no indication that he was willing to go back to port.

The watch officers and the quartermasters hovered around the bridge, waiting for the word. Nerger was downright mysterious. He would pop out of his cabin, take a look at the sky, and pop down again. Not even the stolid Brandes knew what was up. The slender Witschetzky and Leutnant von Oswald, the young Prussian watch officer, stood around and gossiped. When would the captain give the word, so they could keep their dates ashore? They looked at the sky—an ordinary Baltic sky, somewhat better than usual in fact, with patches of blue peeking through the leaden cloud cover. No clue there.

An hour went by. The captain came up, looked at the sky, and went down again. Another hour, and the same performance. The sun began to set, the brilliant orange and purple glinting along the grey green surface of the sea, and then the clouds blew away, and the darkening evening sky was blue. Nerger popped up again, smiled happily, and spoke for the first time in the afternoon.

"We'll stay at sea until tomorrow," he said to Brandes. That was all. The disappointed officers marched glumly down to the mess, cursing their luck, and the word was passed among the crew.

Dawn came, and with it the usual bustle to clear the ship for whatever might be afoot for the day. The ship moved slowly, her engines throbbing gently, and so quietly that the slap of the waves was quite audible to the bow lookout. Then that lookout started, puzzled by a strange buzzing sound overhead, like the drone of a huge, angry bee. He searched the sky, and saw a speck, then a shape, then wings; it was an aeroplane. The plane came over *Wolf*, circled, and landed alongside the port quarter. The officer of the watch went to the speaking tube that led into the captain's cabin and shouted, feeling foolish:

"Aeroplane off the port quarter."

Nerger appeared from his cabin with the cat's smile of one who had known all the time, and issued rapid orders to Brandes. The plane would be hoisted aboard immediately, he said. The two pilots, Leutnants Stein and Fabeck, would be given quarters in officers' country, but when they made port, the aviators were not to go ashore under any circumstances. Nerger unbent a little, to explain.

"They will think the plane has gone on to Travemuende," he confided, "and that's just what we want everyone to think."

So the astonished crew of *Wolf* watched as one of the real loading booms was brought out to port, the hydroplane hooked on, then brought up on deck, where it lay on top of the cargo hatch, dripping incongruously. In a few moments the two pilots had begun directing crewmen in the disassembly of the aircraft, and before the midwatch ended the plane was gone, its parts stowed safely in the mine compartment. *Wolf* was steaming serenely toward her home port, just another innocent merchantman with brown masts, a tall black smokestack, white superstructure, and black hull.

Captain Nerger was making every preparation for his war, and taking no chances.

2

The Breakout

In November, Captain Nerger took the ship to sea again one dark night and by prearrangement met the great minelayer *Deutschland* far out of sight of land, where the only danger might be the eye of a lurking British submarine. Six hundred mines were transferred in the dead of night from the minelayer to the innocent looking merchantman, then the ships parted and made their separate ways back to Kiel, as though they had no business with one another.

Deutschland went out a few days later on her mysterious business, and that left, for the moment, the ship called *Jupiter* as the only one in harbour. The word had been put out that she was a dirty old collier, and that the fire in her had created such complications as to warrant all the naval yard personnel who gave their attention to such a relatively unimportant vessel. Nerger was preoccupied with spies; he felt they were one of the really important weapons that might prevent his success. He was waiting now for a new moon and the darkness it brought; *Jupiter* rode at her lines patiently, bobbing with the tide, but the men of the crew grew tense and expectant as the hour of departure neared. At the end of November all was ready. The ship was literally caked with coal—she was carrying 6,200 tons, crammed into every compartment possible. Guns, ammunition, crew, were all prepared.

On the night of 29 November second in command Brandes issued the orders for the following day: quarters at 6:00 am (they were not standing watches while in harbour), steam up by 10:00; inspection at 10:30, followed by preparation for fire control practice; at 13:30 the ship would steam into Kiel bay and the schooling would begin. All very logical for a ship which had suffered so much from a nearly disastrous coal fire. That evening as the men went ashore they told what they knew, that they were going out next day for the tedious and dull job of learning how to tow targets for other ships' gunners.

Next day, all the crew back safely aboard, Nerger took the ship out through the harbour buoys at seven bells of the midwatch. Soon she passed the signal tower at Bülk, the entrance to Kieler Förde, and made much of sending a message to the target service at Friedrichsort, asking for more

16

targets, announcing that *Jupiter* would be at sea until 4 December on gunnery practice.

It was all for the benefit of the enemy, every bit of it. Nerger was getting ready to try to break through the British blockade of the North Sea and its approaches to the Atlantic. He was headed for the Indian Ocean, with the mission of first laying mines, then beginning the harassment of British shipping wherever he might find it.

On 5 December the unpretentious *Jupiter* crept along through the Kiel canal. Now, headed for the open seas, Leutnant Brandes called all men aft. They lined up, three hundred of them, and Brandes made his announcement. "The gunnery practice story was a ruse . . . we are going to sea and not returning . . . our mission is beginning." Some captains might have made the announcement themselves, but Nerger was not the type to take on heroics; he was concerned only with the job at hand, to strike at the British enemy.

The ship sailed on, the name *Jupiter* now erased from her stern. Out of the canal, Nerger anchored and waited for a submarine which would escort them through the German minefield.* It arrived late in the afternoon, the captain came aboard *Wolf* and he and Nerger repaired to the latter's cabin for half an hour. As

---

* There is some evidence that the German Admiralty planned to send the submarine and surface raider out to work on British shipping in concert, but this matter was never discussed by Captain Nerger either with his officers or in the book he wrote later about his exploits. His silence is perfectly understandable, because the concept was revolutionary, and as the war was still raging when he wrote his book, to tell the story would have been to give aid to the British enemy.

sun set, the pair of vessels moved out through the fields, passed safely, and then the submarine left them. *Wolf* was alone to begin her adventure, armed with her guns, torpedoes, mines, and the *Wölfchen*, the seaplane that would give her far-ranging eyes. The crew was on war watch now, the lookout posts doubly manned, gunners at their guns. By midnight they were off the Danish coast and heading into dangerous waters where their enemy would be the British fleet. Every man was alert.

They passed a Danish post liner, that was all, and the Dane paid them no heed. Why should he? A lumbering collier aroused very little attention in 1916. Nerger moved the ship steadily northward, past Cape Lindesnes, the Norwegian island of Udsire where they saw what appeared to be the smoke from a flotilla of British destroyers—but no destroyers. They passed another freighter, and a flock of fishing boats, and none paid them heed, for Nerger raised the Union Jack and there was nothing more natural in these waters than to see a British merchantman.

The weather, unfortunately, was wonderful, cold but so clear they could see the Norwegian snow peaks in the distance. The submarine that had accompanied them through the minefield had rejoined them, and for a time this created a problem for Nerger. Submerged, the *U-66* could make only about five knots. If they were to keep together as the admiralty had ordered, *Wolf* must slow to five knots, and in this weather every moment wasted was a moment of danger. Nerger weighed the dangers and decided on a course of action. He ordered the submarine to surface and took it in tow, then began moving ahead at eleven knots. A stiff northwest breeze was blowing, straining the tow and kicking up whitecaps in the wake, a welcome development because it half-hid the *U-66* from any prying eyes.

As they moved north, the little convoy was ever more in danger; and soon they would come to the point of decision, where they must move west, one way or another. Between the Shetlands and the Irish coast, the British were constantly on watch. Several warships and auxiliary cruisers patrolled these waters constantly, on the lookout for submarines and blockade runners. The wind changed, then back again, and blew up a gale until the navigator estimated it at Force 10. Neger was very pleased, for the worse the weather the better their chances of breaking through.

Hampered by the tow, he decided on the bold course of moving toward the north, into the Atlantic through the passage between Iceland and Greenland. It meant the danger of icebergs and the terrible freezing storms that coursed these waters, but for every obstacle that nature threw in their way came a concomitant decrease in the chance that they would be discovered by the British. Nerger chose nature.

Waves began to break across the main deck, and to splatter freezing sea up on the bridge, on the masts up to the cross trees, everywhere. The ship pitched and rolled, and the tow line threatened to break as it slackened and snapped tight. The hatches froze shut, the mounts of the guns behind their plating froze, and ice formed on the wire and the upper plates. In the galley the fires went

19

out, and the cooks staggered around their stoves, trying to keep from being burned, trying to keep their stores from collapsing into one great stew. The lookouts picked the icicles from their perches, blew on their mitted hands, and dreamed of vast vats of coffee and flagons of schnapps.

The wind switched around to southwest—and blew even stronger. Nerger estimated it at Force 11 on the Beaufort scale. The textbooks say laconically that force 11 "seldom occurs"—which meant the writers of those books had spent little time in the Arctic waters north of the British Isles. The wind howled, the blizzard came down, and the lookouts could not see anything beyond the ship itself; they were buried in a world of white. By dead reckoning the navigator estimated that they were entering the strait of Denmark. They saw nothing, not even *U-66* which might or might not still be behind them. This was a very dangerous point of the voyage. If the English were out this night, no one could predict what might happen.

But the English were not out on this devil's night, and *Wolf* passed the danger point at 68° latitude, the wind still screaming, the snow still falling, the waves still knocking *Wolf* about like a chip in a tub. The morning of 7 December dawned bright and clear and relatively calm. They could see around them now, but there was nothing to see. The tow line was broken, their tow was gone. Captain Nerger turned the ship about and searched, but there was no sign of *U-66*; whatever had happened, she had left them and there was nothing to do but push on alone. The wind dropped, and they moved on west-northwest through the strait. The sun did not come up until just before noon, stared at them glumly for three hours, and then dropped back behind the horizon. They were far from out of danger.

One of their guns had been damaged by the storm; the gunners were put to work righting things, while the gunners of the others stood nervously at their posts. The torpedo officer fidgeted and checked and rechecked his tubes and warheads. In the radio room, the radio officer listened intently to the transmissions. By now he and his men had come to know several British ships by the technique of their operators; one was very near, as they could tell by the force of the signal. The word went to the bridge, where Captain Nerger fidgeted.

On 9 December the ship awoke to a dead calm, and as the sun came up, again around noon, the crew could see the phantom shapes of icebergs on all sides of them. The transmissions of the British were still very close (representing the British enemy); the thermometer was down around zero (representing the enemy Nature). The guns were covered with a coating of ice three inches thick, and were as useless for battle at the moment as if they had been carved from ice, which was how they appeared. Icicles hung from the stanchions and the rigging, and the decks were thick with ice. But that was the least of Captain Nerger's worries at the moment. Chief Engineer Meyer came up from the engine room with a worried look on his face, headed straight for the captain's cabin, and shut the door firmly behind him. Inside he told Nerger they were in serious trouble below. For a week they had laboured through these heavy seas, the engines breathing in freezing air, and labouring to work. The result was cracked tubes in the boilers, and they had to be replaced before *Wolf* would be able to make anything like her eleven knots again.

Nerger listened and gave the orders. It was 10 December, and they had just reached the open sea, had just broken through the British blockade and were as safe as they would be at any time during the voyage. Let Chief Engineer Meyer shut down the engines then, one at a time, keeping two boilers going while the third was under repair, switching until all the work was done. Meanwhile, here at the edge of the Atlantic, they would stop altogether for two days, giving Meyer a head start on this work, while the crew chipped ice and made the guns ready for action once again.

Wolf was getting ready for action. For a time there would be some relaxation now; the ship could go off war watch, or action stations, and revert to a less demanding routine. Lookouts were posted fore and aft and on the bridge. Two officers were constantly on the bridge, the officer of the watch and the navigator; but the rest could take it easy for a while. It had been a serious strain on men and ship to run the blockade, even though it had taken only ten days, and Captain Nerger was glad to give the crew a little respite. He knew better than they that the strain was only beginning, and he intended to make this a long and successful voyage against the enemy.

So the ship settled down. As they moved south, the sun shone warmly down on them. The men were not idle, for there was much to be done. For one thing, *Wolf* had to change her appearance, lest some of those neutrals she had passed in the breakout should remember her and connect the ship with a raider in mid-ocean. So the paintpots were brought out, and the white of the superstructure disappeared under a dirty brown.

3

South to Africa—and Beyond

They took the sun route, the men of *Wolf*. By 16 December, they were approximately opposite the chill highlands of Scotland; ten days later they were west of Madeira, and Christmas was spent in the neighbourhood of Cape Verde where the sun almost always shines. They saw a few ships, the first when the *Wolf* cut across the sealane that leads from Britain to American and Canadian ports, but they let them go on their way unmolested. Captain Nerger's business was to be conducted in another place, and besides, just after their breakthrough they learned that the famous *Möwe* was out ahead of them, Dohna-Schlodien having begun his second raiding cruise. To stir the world right here in the middle of the North Atlantic would bring the wolf-hunters of Britain running, and that is not what Nerger wanted at all. He had his mines to deliver before undertaking any other task. So as the smoke of other ships appeared on the horizon, Nerger ordered changes of course, appearing to sail somewhere in particular, either toward the new world, or the old. As for himself, Nerger now spent a bit of time with his books. He had made sure that the library of *Wolf* was well-stocked with the great books of Germany, the philosophers and the literary lights as well as the historians and advisers on warfare. There was something for every taste, and for a change—for a little while—there was opportunity to indulge.

When the ship crossed the equator, Nerger was relaxed enough to permit the traditional ceremonies in honour of Neptunus Rex, which involved elaborate horseplay by the old hands of the crew, and a considerable amount of refined torture for the "pollywogs." They were oiled, covered with coal dust, thoroughly doused in sea water, and baptized in the name of the king of the sea. Then there was a huge feast aboard *Wolf* for everyone; in the crew's messes there was beer and extra rations of cigarettes; the officers ate a pair of ducks that had been brought aboard for a special occasion such as this, and drank champagne, then smoked their cigars with a feeling of immense satisfaction.

Moving down the South Atlantic, the voyage became actually boring. In the northern waters there was always something to see, mostly English and allied ships, to be sure, but at least distraction. Here in the south, days went by when not a single

26

object crossed the blue expanses of sea and sky. For officers and men it was dull, day after day, and they did not even have a particular sense of mission, for Captain Nerger kept his orders to himself and no one else knew where they were going or what they were to do.

On 16 January the ship approached the Cape of Good Hope, albatrosses circling, and Nerger unbent enough to inform his officers that they were going to lay mines off the cape. They came in quietly toward the land, slowing so they would reach their destined waters well after dark, when the danger of exposure was least, and just before nightfall a lookout sighted the bump on the horizon that meant land. A little later the lookouts sighted half a dozen smoke plumes, and as they came up on the starboard, Nerger and his men saw they were led by a big cruiser flying the White Ensign. The convoy ignored the black ship, obviously thinking it was a friendly merchantman, and the smoke trailed on past them, to dissipate in the gathering darkness.

Night fell with the suddenness of a theatre curtain, as it does in the tropics, and *Wolf* embraced the darkness for it lent a margin of safety to the work that Nerger wanted. The mines were to be laid inside the fifty fathom line, just off the coast, for here was the steamer lane. In the bows the lookouts began sounding, and on the bridge Nerger took command himself for the delicate operation. The mine officer was at his post as the ship crept in, one of his men wearing earphones and waiting for the orders from the bridge.

"Eighty fathoms," came the voice from the bridge.

27

"Seventy fathoms."

"Sixty fathoms . . ." droned the talker.

They moved in toward the land, and the water they would mine.

The ship they had seen that day was *Cornwall*, leading six transports loaded with troops who were heading north for the war. The British were very much on the alert, particularly for surface raiders. *Möwe* was loose in the South Atlantic, taking prizes and being hunted across the sea, near the South American coast. The cruisers *Kent* and *Hyacinth* were assigned to the Cape command, and Whitehall had just ordered *Hyacinth* to remain in the waters around the cape, postponing a visit to East Africa which had been scheduled much earlier, before the current panic began.

That night Nerger moved into shallow water, off Dassen Island, in Saldhana Bay. As they came inshore, they could see the lights of the port there, silhouetting a handful of ships in harbour. A searchlight played across the sea, and another sought it out, but they paid no attention to *Wolf*, and she moved steadily toward shore, zig-zagging, her mine-laying begun. She laid some thirty mines there that night, and then headed back out to sea and comparative safety. Two nights later, *Wolf* was inshore again, laying mines on the steamer route south of Cape Agulhas; this done, Captain Nerger moved out of the steamer lanes and headed east. The men of *Wolf* knew nothing more than that. They had no idea their captain was taking them to the Indian Ocean.

Wolf had long left the area when the first results of her efforts became known. On 25 January, the British freighters *Matheran* and *Portugal*

28

moved unsuspectingly into the waters off Dassen Island, and into trouble. *Matheran* hit a mine and sank; *Portugal* was luckier: she had a huge hole in her, but managed to stay afloat and was towed back to Simon's Bay, where the word went out that she had been torpedoed. That word was transmitted by radio to London, South America, and all the ships at sea. With great delight the radiomen of *Wolf* listened to the warnings that German U-boats must be patrolling off the Cape of Good Hope. Even Nerger's stern face opened up in a smile at that misinformation from the enemy. He would have laughed outright, had he known what a sweat the British were in: next day the navy stopped a Swedish ship in Cape Town harbour, virtually accused the captain of being in cahoots with the Germans, and searched his ship from top to bottom, finding nothing. In the panic airplanes circled the waters endlessly, the cruisers and lesser ships steamed at high speed along the coast, binoculars flashing in the sun, wasting tons of coal and ready to fire at anything that moved in the water. All transports sailing for South Africa from England and South America were stopped wherever they might be. It was a week before the truth came out, a week loaded with every kind of rumour, from the story of the "submarine" to a flat statement that both ships had been the victims of internal explosions. Then, when the truth emerged, the fifty-five ships of the Cape, East Indies, and China commands were all alerted to look for a new raider somewhere at sea—no one quite knew where. The confusion was heightened on 10 February when the minefield off Cape Agulhas was discovered. By this time *Wolf* was at 60° E, having headed straight eastward from the cape after her adventures in destruction, and Nerger was moving against a new target.

Wolf was a German warship, and the fact was never forgotten, no matter how ill-kept or raunchy she might appear from a distance, as she chose to do. The crew were on their toes, and kept there by the stern discipline of the German navy. The smokestack was raked a little, the paint colour changed on the upper works as they moved along, partly to keep the men busy, partly to further confuse anyone who might come into sight. The watchkeepers were kept alert by the captain himself, who might come up out of his cabin at any hour of day or night to see how affairs were progressing. On 27 January, the crew celebrated the Kaiser's birthday with all the pomp of which *Wolf* was capable—another disciplinary measure. Nerger made one of his rare speeches, telling the men that theirs was a special task, that they must strain every nerve to sink enemy ships and bring honour to the Emperor and the nation. He spoke of the need for tenacity and patience, and self-control during the long voyage that lay ahead of them. It was the first that some men knew about the purpose of their trip; he did not exactly tell them, but in his words was the warning that much lay ahead of them and they must prepare themselves to face adversity. There was plenty of fresh fruit, plenty of tobacco still aboard, but the indication was that this might not always be so, and still they must prevail. The men met his words as he expected, with three great cheers for the Kaiser, and the assemblage broke up. In the afternoon the men gathered again on the afterdeck, but this time in a spirit of frolic. A group of sailors from the Tyrol gave a concert. Then the ship's wrestling competition began, and before the day was over a champion, Seaman Wenzel, had been crowned.

Out here in the vastness of the ocean, the chief engineer asked permission to stop the ship for a day to complete the repairs to his boilers, and Captain Nerger agreed. While the black gang laboured below, Nerger sent Brandes and Leutnant Witschetzky off in a launch to move around the ship and check their camouflage. They went slowly, looking at every detail, and returned to report that no sign could be seen of guns or any equipment that would tell the world *Wolf* was something other than what she pretended to be.

Then came a dirty job; movement of coal from the cargo holds down into the fire room and bunkers. The men put on their oldest fatigue uniforms, and began the parade, loading sacks with coal, carrying them to the bunkers, dumping them, climbing back up and repeating the process. It was hot, the tropical sun baked them on deck and made an oven of the steel plates of the coal hold. The wind died down and it was absolutely calm, which removed the one great benefit of the sea in hot weather; still the men laughed and sang as they worked. After the repair was finished, the coaling went on. For six days *Wolf* travelled in a cloud of coal dust, the grime penetrated every cranny of the ship, and when it was over, there was as much work in hosing down and cleaning up as there had been in movement of the coal. It was a tremendous task, this kind of coaling, but accepted as necessary by a captain who knew he had no place to turn for the precious fuel except to capture it. There was virtually no neutral territory between him and home, and if he came across a neutral ship, he might expect (and did) that it would turn out to exhibit a very dubious neutrality once the German ship was out of sight, and that his position would almost immediately be made known to the British admiralty.

The radioman kept getting word about the *Möwe* indirectly in listening to the in-the-clear broadcasts of the British, warning ships at sea about the presence of the raider off the South American coast. *Wolf*'s existence was still unknown to the British, largely by reason of Nerger's intense precautions beginning on the day the ship was bought and commissioned by the Imperial Navy. As he headed for Ceylon now, Britain tried to strengthen her network in the far east, feeling something was up, but not quite knowing what it was. The admiralty sent reinforcements eastward. The cruiser *Newcastle* headed for Colombo; the Japanese promised to send two cruisers to the Indian Ocean, and the French were asked for three ships. One of the worries of the admiralty was the large number of German ships in harbour in the Dutch East Indies, which were neutral, and the possibility that an alert German navy might try to arm these ships and break them out as commerce raiders.

As the *Wolf* headed north toward the equator, the heat grew worse, and the officers took to their hammocks, too hot even to talk. There was more than normal heat, the wind died down, the sea became glassy, and Captain Nerger prepared himself for a hurricane—he knew the signs. Sure enough,

on 8 February the glass began to fall and dropped
out of sight, the sun shone red, and then the
clouds moved in, big, black threatening clouds
that seemed to descend on the ship, bent on ven-
geance.

The wind began to blow, soft and cool at first,
and then rising in tempo until it screamed
through the steel rigging. The sea rose up in an-
ger, blue turning to an angry green and then to
grey, the tops of the waves lashed furiously into
spume, the salt spray charging the bridge and
slapping the faces of the lookouts and the watch.
The hurricane battered the ship for half an hour,
and then everything suddenly stopped; the sea
grew calm, and the wind died down; the rain
stopped pelting *Wolf*. Captain Nerger was not
fooled. They had just had half of it—they were in
the eye of the hurricane, and must ride out another beating. Such storms have sunk many a ship,
and this one smashed *Wolf* hard enough to bend
plates and twist stanchions, but the ship came
through it well, as well as it had survived the terrible icy storms of the breakthrough above
Iceland.

The storm over, Captain Nerger concentrated
his men on damage repair, getting ready for his
next venture, which would be the mining of the
waters off Ceylon. His plan was to arrive off Colombo on the evening of 15 February, the night of
the new moon. That would give him darkness in
which to work, to sow mines that should account
for more enemy ships, for the route from the Far
East home to Britain lay around Ceylon, and particularly in these war days nearly all ships hugged

the safety of the British lanes and bases when they could.

The British at Colombo had been quite put off by the events of the last few weeks, and particularly the confusion that resulted from the extraordinarily successful raiding of Count Dohna-Schlodien, in *Möwe*. Vice-Admiral W. L. Grant of the China Station was sorely pressed to try to cover all his area with a handful of vessels of various degrees of efficiency.

The cruiser *Sapphire* with her twelve 4 inch guns, was in Colombo harbour, but she was laid up refitting. The *City of London*, which could make fifteen knots and carried eight 6 inch guns, was in Colombo, too, and she was ready for action. As for the other ships of Admiral Grant's command, they were scattered, as the navy men would say, from Hell to breakfast; at Hong Kong, Bombay, and Singapore, with the four Japanese cruisers that had just joined the force either in Singapore or heading there. Vice-Admiral Sir Rosslyn Wemyss, commander of the East Indies force, had the feeling that a new armed raider was moving around in his area, but it was no more than a feeling; it could be quite false, and he could not play with his forces on the basis of a hunch. So while he had just ordered *Sapphire* to snap up that refit and then begin patrol of the western approaches to Colombo instead of going back to Aden as was the old plan, there was no terrible sense of urgency that night.

As Captain Nerger moved inshore in the gathering darkness, the lights of Colombo and the countryside around began to flicker, and against them he could see the vague outlines of several ships in

34

the harbour and at the quay. He would expect at least a handful of patrol boats to be out at evening, covering the mouth of the harbour if nothing else, and as the crew moved to battle stations, Nerger peered into the darkness, looking for the phosphorescence of a bow wave or a wake. But there was nothing, no sign of life at all on the sea around the naval base. The British were sound asleep.

Nerger was taking no chances. He gave his instructions from the bridge. The gunnery officer and the torpedo officer were to be ready for action at any moment. They were not to open fire unless discovered, then they were to sink the enemy ship immediately. This understood, Nerger ordered the mine-laying to begin, and *Wolf* zig-zagged through the approaches to the deep water harbour, dropping some twenty round steel balls, whose long horns waited for the scraping of a ship's bottom to set off the frightful explosion. In a few hours the job was finished, and Captain Nerger set course northward for Bombay harbour, where he intended to do precisely the same.

On 19 February, in the daylight hours, *Wolf* encountered a good deal of traffic on the lane from Colombo to Bombay, but moved away each time smoke appeared and was never seriously challenged. That evening the ship neared the harbour of the great port city, and prepared to lay mines again. The men were at action stations when the word came:

"Ship, blacked out, on the starboard bow."

Blacked out meant a warship, and a warship meant trouble and possible fight to the death. The men stood quiet, the only sounds being the creaking of the ship, the pounding of the engines, and the words of the talkers as they read off the range and speed of the coming target.

Would he come in, the enemy? He would not; having looked over *Wolf* from a distance, the patrolling vessel heeled sharply and sped away on some other business, satisfied that here was just another plodding merchantman. *Wolf* was left in peace to sow her deadly eggs, and did so in the dark of the night, finished and away two hours before dawn, heading for the Karachi area with the intention of doing the same once again.

The British were not as sound asleep as Nerger had hoped they might be. The Bombay minefield was discovered next morning and the alert was sounded. *Wolf*'s radio operators caught the signals from the naval forces, warning all ships to beware of mines and look out for enemy vessels. So for the moment the mining game was over, it would be too dangerous to approach any Indian port within the next few weeks. *Wolf* had to find another way to make her presence known and damage the British enemy.

4

The Lonely Life of the Corsair

In the modern annals of the sea there is no experience that quite matches up to that of the German raiders of World War I for sheer adventure, in the ancient traditions of the sea, and the exploits of *Wolf* and her sister raiders will never be repeated. For one thing, by the spring of 1917 even World War I had changed so drastically that sea warfare was revolutionized; the major agent of change was the submarine, whose deadly work had to be done, if it was to be most effective, without warning. The old tradition of the sea held that men did not kill the innocent, which meant the crews of freighters and the passengers of ships. Seamen like von Luckner, von Müller, and Dohna-Schlodien lived up to the knightly traditions of seafaring men of ages past: make war on warriors. But the German naval strategy after Jutland had to be changed. No matter what damage the high seas fleet had inflicted on the British, Jutland had left England in control of European waters and the German general staff knew it very well. The entrance of America into the war was almost certain if the submarine campaign continued, but the generals and the admirals calculated the risk, decided that at all costs they must stop the British from creating their new war machine, and the submarine campaign of unrestricted warfare was on. It set the tradition, in the winter of 1916–17, of a new kind of warfare that would persist into the Second World War.

Wolf was then an anomaly even as she steamed into the heartland of the enemy's empire, laying her mines. But she and her captain and crew were of the old tradition yet, sailing out from home, out of sight of any friendly faces; out of contact with their world, for the high speed, powerful radios and communications network that now reach around the globe were yet to come. At sea Nerger travelled under his orders, but he was in charge and his actions were left to his discretion. There would be raiders in the Second World War, but quite different sorts of raiders; their voyages controlled from start to finish by staff officers back at their desks in Germany; the logistics of supply met by a complex combination of surface fuelling vessels and submarines. Not so in February 1917. Nerger and his three hundred German warriors were alone, in the old tradition of the sea. Whether they survived or died depended on themselves; what course they took, where they operated and how, was up to the captain, and no one would gainsay him, as the Nazis would do to later raider captains of the Second World War. Nerger and Müller and Dohna were of the Drake tradition, out laying the enemy waste on behalf of crown and country.

In the quiet of his cabin, Karl Nerger liked to put down the cares of the day, and lying on his bunk, cigar in hand, would peruse the works of Kant and Hegel, his favourite philosophers. In the hours of leisure that seemed to come in stacks, this was how he whiled away his time, for a captain must remain aloof; the philosophers helped him bear his lonely lot, and his reading kept him from prowling the bridge and the working places of the ship, where it was often best that he should not know precisely how his orders were carried out, in the interest of good company morale. But now the philosophers were set aside; Karl Nerger had new concerns and the crew must be made to respond to a new set of problems. If they were to be effective, now the minelaying had been discovered, they would have to conduct what the French call *la guerre de course*—the hit and run raiding of the corsair, finding a victim, surprising him, taking him, and then deciding what would be done with the booty of war, whether to send it to the bottom or to try to make some other use of it on behalf of his Imperial Majesty.

The news, picked up from the radio, that Bombay port was closed until further notice because of mines, brought about the change, no matter what Nerger might have wanted—for the word was also passed that no ships were to approach the coast within the hundred fathom curve, and that meant mining would not only be dangerous but ineffective. For the moment the wise course was to move out of coastal waters altogether, to pause and consider when and where the next move should come. Nerger ordered the navigator to plot a course south-southwest, and headed down the Indian Ocean between the Indian and Arab peninsulas.

On 24 February, *Wolf* reached the sealane that runs between Aden and Bombay. These hot days were spent in training, running out the guns against a stopwatch, practice firing (without ammunition, for a raider had no shells to waste on practice), and the timing of the precious seconds it took the crew to reach their action stations. In an attack, time would be the essential factor, for some if not all the quarry to be sought would carry radios and would try to send messages to other ships at sea and the British navy. The radios must be stopped, and speed in getting the guns unlimbered was the essential factor. To test them, Nerger ordered action stations at any time: a drill might come at four bells on the night watch, when half the crew were sound asleep in their hammocks. Or it might come at three bells on the day watch, when the warm breezes had caused the men to relax. Night watch, midwatch, dogwatch— it made no difference to Nerger, for he knew that their very lives depended on the cat's speed in striking for survival.

Nerger steamed on, mindful of the dangers. So far his cruise had not been unsuccessful in a modest way; two ships out of action off the African coast, and now came the word that the seven thousand ton liner *Worcestershire* had struck one of

Wolf's mines off Colombo and had sunk. Captain Nerger was much amused by the messages picked up on the air. At first the authorities said *Worcestershire* had sunk after "an internal explosion." Internal explosion indeed, caused by what the British referred to as Nerger's "infernal machine." Seven miles off Colombo—that was enough for Nerger to know how effective his "Hollenmaschine" had been. And then he heard that a second ship, *Perseus*, the same size as *Worcestershire*, had also gone down. (British records did not show it thus.) Nerger also learned of the wickedness of his British enemy. After the disaster the people on board, as with the *Worcestershire*, were brought to Colombo. All the passengers and crew were segregated, kept away from British and Indians alike, so that the public would not learn of the success of the infernal machines. The British, Nerger said, simply could not stand this blow to their dignity and concealed it. This success made Nerger very happy. There were no pleasanter words to his ears than the simple statement: *"Der Hafen ist geschlossen"* (The port is closed). He was also very pleased, later, to discover that at Bombay the P&O liner *Mongolia* had run afoul of his minefield.

Nerger now found himself in waters where no German war vessel had ventured since the death of the *Emden* in the early days of the war. This was a vast span of sea, extending from the shores of India on the north, to the Antarctic waters thousands of miles south, and from the coast of East Africa and Madagascar to Australia and the East Indies. In the north and centre of this huge area the British ran a steady stream of traffic to supply their war effort in Europe and maintain control of the far-flung Asian colonies. For a raider, this was all opportunity; even if Captain Nerger could not guarantee a supply of coal from friendly forces, here in the Indian Ocean he could find safe havens among the lonely islands that dotted the sea, at a pinch he could commandeer coal from an island dump, and he would find good hunting among the merchantmen. As for enemies, the battle cruiser *Euryalus* was still refitting at Bombay, *Dufferin* was in drydock there, the little *Suva* with only three 4.7 inch guns was at sea, as were two or three other ships of a class that *Wolf* really need not fear much, for she was better armed. It would take a real alarm, a true fright, to put the British out so much that they would concentrate the fragile defences of the area in search for a single raider.

Nerger headed first for the ship lane that runs between Colombo and Aden, one of the lifelines of the Empire. On 24 February *Wolf* reached the area, and the captain announced that the first man to sight a quarry would get ten extra cigarettes, a promise that sharpened eyes and sent lookouts clambering eagerly to their posts.

The first day, nothing, and the second. But on the morning of 27 February came a shout from the forward lookout:

"Steamer three points off the port bow."

The officer of the watch called the captain, and Nerger came hurrying to the bridge.

What was that ship? He considered. It was most unlikely to be a neutral, in these waters in this year of war. He could not call her up on the radio—the radio was his worst enemy, and he must

42

presume that if the other had the slightest inkling he was a German that she would use her radio, if she had one. Nerger looked carefully through his glasses. The stack, the shape, the whole rigging— she must be a British ship, he would swear to it. He gave the order to turn *Wolf* on an intercepting course, and to pour on the coal.

As soon as *Wolf* turned, and began making more smoke, the other ship began to run for it. But she was obviously homeward bound from her voyage, and laden with the dusty soft coal of these tropical parts, while *Wolf* was blessed yet with the good, hard, hot-burning product of the Ruhr. Swiftly, *Wolf* drew up on her quarry, even as the other ship sent a long black trail of smoke into the sky in her haste. By eight o'clock in the morning, *Wolf* drew up on her after a three-hour chase, during which Nerger had stayed planted on that bridge of his as if his feet grew there. As they closed, the captain ordered the signal:

"Stop immediately. I am sending a boat."

Wolf moved up to a point a thousand yards off the other ship's stern. From the other ship, she still seemed to be a big merchantman, but the naval crew of *Wolf* had been at action stations for four hours. Behind their false fronts, the seven guns were manned, and the four torpedo tubes were ready. On the main deck, the boarding party was assembling: two officers in their colonial whites, wearing swords and pistols, a petty officer and ten sailors carrying rifles with bayonets fixed. Leutnant Rose was in command, for he spoke English fluently. The signal flags flapped briskly in the breeze, the boarding party made ready, as *Wolf* moved up so that Captain Nerger could

43

check his hunch. There it was on the stern: *Turritella* in big white letters, and just a little smaller, below the name, the word *London*.

Aboard *Wolf* there was still silence, and only a few heads showed. The crew of Number Four gun stuck up their eyes over the plating, to catch a glimpse of the action, and Leutnant Witschetzky cursed and shouted at them to get their heads down before he blew them off. The offenders ducked.

Aboard the *Turritella* Nerger could see the captain on the bridge and men scurrying to and fro; but she did not stop. The captain decided to try to run for it, and the ship gave a little surge forward as *Wolf* slowed down.

Nerger saw, and reacted.

"Fire a shot across her bow," he ordered.

Leutnant Witschetzky passed the order: "On the starboard, there, Gun Number Two, put a shell across her."

The gun fired, the shell passed low over the bridge, and plopped into the sea, with the unmistakable splash of destruction. Just then the *Wolf*'s boat was away, the *Wolf*'s war flag running up masthead, the white ensign of Imperial Germany, with the black maltese cross in the corner, superimposed on the red, white and black national flag, the eagle of the Emperor on the centre. The other ship was flying the red ensign, the British merchantman's flag, with its Union Jack superimposed on the crimson banner, and for a few minutes more the flag flew bravely, defiantly in the face of what the British captain now knew as his enemy. Aboard the *Turritella* men scurried about, pulling on life-jackets, expecting to be sent into their boats, or worse, into the sea itself.

Leutnant Rose and his boarding party moved swiftly across the six hundred yards that separated the ships, and Rose demanded a ladder. It was thrown down, he scampered up pistol in hand and headed immediately for the mast, where he hauled down the Union Jack and hauled up the German ensign. The second officer headed for the bridge, where he informed the captain he was a prisoner. The petty officer went down the companionway to the engine room, making sure that the ship's engineer did not try to sabotage the engines. Rose came to the bridge, and sent the others on a search of the officer's cabins for arms. In five minutes all the guns were assembled, and the crew, mostly Chinese, were under control. Oddly enough, as Rose examined the papers of the *Turritella*, he discovered that she was the sister ship of *Wolf*. The English ship was in truth the Hansa vessel *Gutenfels*, which had been captured at the outbreak of war by British auxiliary cruisers off Port Said.

Rose and the others were a little slow in passing the word to Nerger, and the captain grew impatient. What ship was this? he signalled. Where was she going and where was she coming from? Rose hastened to reply, and a signalman began waving his flags on the bridge of the prize: *Turritella*—5,528 tons, carrying eight hundred tons of coal (one could almost see Nerger smile), oil for the British fleet and supplies for the British army in the Middle East, bound from Colombo to England by way of Salonika. Briskly, Captain Nerger now gave his orders. He told Leutnant Rose to

45

bring *Turritella* around astern of Wolf and fall in line; they would now head south, away from the steamer lane, so their business would not be observed by unwanted watchers.

Rose found something among the papers that interested him, and he knew would interest the captain; not the secret codes of the British navy, for Captain Meadows, a big, burly New Zealander, had already destroyed those and the other papers that he thought might help the Germans; but there was evidence of the effectiveness of the minefields, newspapers from Colombo, and even better, a lifeboat from *Worcestershire* which had been picked up floating, abandoned at sea, off Colombo. Captain Meadows had neglected to destroy the handful of newspapers, quite forgetting how important they would be to the Germans. Triumphantly Rose took the captain and the first mate of *Turritella* with him back to the bridge of *Wolf*.

"Why didn't you stop when ordered?" asked Nerger coldly. "I could have you shot for violation of the rules of war."

"I was taking a nap in the bathtub," said Meadows.

"I didn't understand what you wanted," said the mate.

And of course, although Nerger shook his head in disgust, there was nothing he could do about that.

The news from Rose that *Turritella* was really another *Wolf* was very exciting to the captain of the raider. He began thinking immediately of ways in which he might make use of this remarkable find. Suddenly it came to him: he would put a German crew aboard her, and use her as an auxiliary minelayer and cruiser. It would not take so much—the Chinese crew had no stake in this war and they would serve as well under the Germans as they had under the English; indeed, both navies in the far east had used Chinese for years; it was six of one and half a dozen of the other to the men from Canton and Shanghai and Kiaochow bay. So the work was begun. *Turritella* was carrying, among other things, a large cargo of tinned pineapple, which delighted the Germans. The ship's pineapples were replaced with fruit of another kind, some twenty-five mines which were to be laid in the road off Aden. This was done when the two ships stopped a few miles south of the Aden-Colombo lanes, and the prize crew brought *Turritella* alongside *Wolf*. Lines were passed, the ships were drawn up together with hawsers snaked down between to keep the plates from rubbing and smashing.

She would be christened *Iltis*, declared Captain Nerger, in honour of the German gunboat which had just recently been destroyed after a long and worthy career. *Iltis*—the old one—had represented the Emperor in the action off Taku bar at the time of the Boxers, and had served nobly in the East Asia squadron even as she aged. Further, Captain Nerger had served in her in those long-gone days, as a very junior officer, a happy-go-lucky ensign discovering the mysteries of the far east.

From the crew of three hundred, Nerger chose twenty-seven men to take over the new *Iltis* and carry the war into British waters. Kapitänleutnant Brandes would become the commander. Nerger

47

was not eager to lose his second in command, but the mission was too important, the opportunity too great, to entrust to a lesser figure on the ship. With his usual efficiency, the smiling Brandes took over this newest of his Imperial Majesty's warships. Rifles, pistols, and ammunition were loaded as the pineapples came off. A five centimetre gun was mounted, to give *Iltis* teeth, a crude minelaying device was rigged up to help the ship do her new job and out of the hold came a portable wireless station for the warship.

Nerger was always a very careful man. Now he ordered pilots Fabeck and Stein into the *Wölfchen*, the seaplane and aloft to circle around *Iltis* and discover her deficiencies, if any. They climbed to six thousand feet, and then came down for a close look. All was fine. Then they went back up, and circled, watching for enemy ships that might try to disturb this armament job, for while transferring all these people and supplies, *Wolf* was at her most vulnerable. But with *Wölfchen* around to protect the mother ship, it was a different story.

All afternoon the work went on, and *Wölfchen* came back for gas and went aloft again. Finally, about 7:30 pm the job was done, and Germany had her new warship. The two German crews lined the decks, and cheered each other and the Kaiser and the captain. Meadows, the British captain, looked on gloomily as his ship was stolen away from him. "The Germans are bastards from head to toe," he said with some heat and he offered to bet one of the German officers that inside two weeks the whole jig would be up, and *Wolf*, too, would be destroyed. There were no takers. *Il-*

tis headed west then, disappearing into the gathering gloom of night, while *Wolf* pointed her way back north, toward the Colombo-Aden lanes, looking for more game.

"At least they didn't get any coal," said Meadows with some satisfaction, and he made a point of telling the boarding officers that if they were looking for coal on the Colombo-Aden run they were on the wrong track. But Meadows did not know how determined Nerger was to stay at sea, how he would search high and low, and accept almost any hardship.

There were some rough edges aboard *Wolf*, and the captain chose this day to iron a few of them out. Kapitänleutnant Schmehl, a merchant officer and reservist, had been chosen to take over the duties as executive, and early in the morning, Nerger called for him. He had noticed the behaviour of the men after the capture of the British ship, Nerger said with a scowl, and he did not like it. There was a lot of looting, and he would not have it. The men were called up to the afterdeck. Nerger put on his most official frown and stepped forward. The crew had been guilty of looting, he said, and in time of war, this was punishable by death. He would have no more of it. Everything that was stolen from the British was to be returned, and even the cases of pineapples which the men had put down in their messes were to be taken to stores. All this belonged to the German state, and there would be no next time.

The prisoners, now confined most of the time to the hold where the first batches of mines had been stored, soon learned that while they were captives, they were going to be treated properly, if not over-gently. From time to time German officers tried to get a little information out of Meadows and his officers, but Meadows simply said he would not talk. He set about planning ways he could carry on the war against the enemy.

Back on the sea lane, *Wolf* was not so very lucky. The lookouts spotted one ship just on the horizon, but she was a big liner, much too fast, and there was not even any point in giving chase. A few hours later another smoke plume was seen, but heading on a course so difficult to intercept that Captain Nerger decided not to undertake the stern chase. Every decision he made now was made with one end in view: to inflict maximum damage on the enemy, with minimum danger to his ship and crew.

5

Time is the Enemy

Every morning at dawn, Pilot Stein or Pilot Fabeck reported to the bridge, and the little hydroplane was lifted over the side of *Wolf*, the pilot gunned the engine in the almost glassy sea, the hot exhaust poured out behind the plane into the warming air of another tropical day, the seaplane lifted, circled, and the day's hunt began. "The capture of the *Turritella* had whetted our appetites," wrote Captain Nerger, and now the men were doubly alert and eager, searching for quarry.

The searches were not in vain. In the grey light of dawn on 1 March, the watch spotted a bit of smoke, and the order to action stations rang out through the ship. Leutnant Witschetzky, the gunnery officer, gave the order to arm the guns. A moment later there was an explosion, and flame shot up astern from the platform of gun Number Four. Witschetzky rushed aft, meeting on the deck a string of bloody, blackened men. One man crawled on his hands, useless legs trailing; he dropped, and died. Two others followed, one holding hands to his bleeding eyes, the second clutching his bleeding chest.

The shot had come from gun Number Three, fired by accident, and it had exploded in the ammunition locker of Number Four, at the rear of the bridge, smashing everything, from lifeboats to men. The chase was on, Nerger had no time to stop and find out why the accident had occurred, for he was pressing after this new steamer. The ship's two doctors took the wounded and dying into the sick bay, the damage control parties set to work.

Wolf pulled up on the other vessel, and the captain gave the order for the warning shot. The gun boomed out again, purposefully this time, and the shell went skipping across the sea. But instead of stopping, the other ship turned in a half circle and headed for *Wolf*. Nerger shouted an order from the bridge.

"All engines, full back."

The telegraph clanged, the tempo of the engines slowed, and changed, and the screw thrashed as it reversed direction in the frothy water. From the bridge Nerger now could see that the upper works of the other ship were vacant. Captain and crew had left the bridge, heading for the lifeboats, and the ship was sailing herself. Another shot, closer this time, made someone realize that the *Wolf* must be heard and obeyed, and as the German war flag and signals to stop flashed up the mast of *Wolf*, the other ship's engines came to a halt. The crew, clambering into the lifeboats, quieted and waited for the boarding party, and order was restored. Rose was quick this time to report to the captain, having heard in some detail what might happen if there were a repetition of the delays that had marked the capture of the *Turritella*. This ship, he reported, was the British freighter *Jumna*, carrying a cargo of salt from Spain to Calcutta. That cargo was of no use, but the coal aboard the *Jumna* could be utilized, so Nerger ordered Rose to bring her alongside without delay, and the transfer of the fuel began.

It took two days to move the three hundred tons of Cardiff coal from captive to captor, and during this period the captain set about discovering what had happened to bring so much trouble to his ship with the misfiring of the shell. It had struck in an ammunition storage compartment, setting fire to fifteen grenades, which caused most of the damage. It had just missed a torpedo warhead, and if it had hit home there the whole ship might have gone up in smoke. Seaman Frenz had saved the day, it was learned, picking up the box of burning grenades and throwing them overboard even as they exploded. He had survived, but Quarter-masters Stüven and Bruder were dead, twenty-four men were wounded, ten of them very seriously, and the doctors predicted gloomily that three or four more were going to die.

The coaling stopped long enough for a military funeral; the German war flag was laid tenderly over the two white forms sewn in their sacks, and then the long objects slid into the sea as the crew sang *Ich hatt' einen Kameraden* ... the sad song of lament for a dead comrade that had seized Germany in these unhappy years, and second in command Schmehl read a few words from the Bible. Then it was back to work in the grime of the *Jumna*'s coal hold, while the officers moved about the enemy ship, collecting navigation equipment and any other useful material they could find.

Second-class Armourer Beierl died that night, and was buried even as the men of *Wolf* prepared to send *Jumna* to join their comrades. The thirty-one Englishmen and one Portuguese seaman were taken aboard the raider and sent down to the holds, the officers to join Captain Meadows and his officers, the men to join the seamen of the *Turritella*. As darkness fell, all had deserted *Jumna* save Hilfsleutnant zur See Dietrich, mine officer of the *Wolf*, who was also given the duty of demolishing of all the captured ships that had to be sunk.

Charges were set in the engine room and on the bridge. Dietrich lit the fuse, then scurried over the side into the boat manned by his restless crew. They pulled hard for *Wolf*; halfway across the thousand yards between ships there came a tremendous explosion that shook the boat, and a column of water shot up alongside the starboard beam of the stricken ship; smoke belched out of her chimney, and she nosed down. Soon the bridge was awash, and jetsam was breaking away

54

from her upper works. A lifeboat detached itself
from the bridgeworks, irritating, because it had to
be run down and sunk lest the presence of *Wolf*
be made known by such bones of her captives.
Then came a gurgle and a swirl, and the salt of
Spain joined the salt of the sea.

To bring home the horrors of the war, another
man died next day, torpedoman Hampe, who had
been injured in the accident. But there was no
stopping the war, or the duty imposed on captain
and crew to wage it here halfway around the
world from home. And Captain Nerger's mind was
occupied with current worries: his engines were
foul and his boilers dirty after all this travel; they
needed an overhaul and in the interim they
wasted fuel, cast up black smoke that might give
away *Wolf*'s position to an enemy, and cut down
the speed that always was essential for pursuit or
flight. There was much to be done, the ship still
carried some two hundred mines that ought to be
laid in the path of the enemy, and there were
more merchantmen to be captured. What was
wanted was a big fat coaler from Cardiff. Nerger
had to have some such, or he would never get
home at all. Privately, in the quiet of his cabin, he
smoked his cigars, read his Kant, and worried.

5 March came, the day that Kapitänleutnant
Brandes was to lay his mines outside Aden. Had
he succeeded? The word came by radio next day.
Wolf's operator gleefully intercepted the welcome
message: *Notice to ships at sea. The Aden roads
have been mined. German raider in the Indian
Ocean.* Whether this last meant *Iltis* or *Wolf* was a
little vague. Captain Nerger hoped the British

might believe *Iltis* was *Wolf*, there was certainly good enough reason for the confusion since their hull lines were almost precisely the same. For a while at least, he could imagine the Admiralty in confusion. But what was happening to *Iltis?* It would be some time before Nerger would learn, sadly, that Brandes had been surprised by the British.

Brandes had done well enough, in the beginning, *Iltis* had steamed along, and laid her mines. But that night, the senior officer present at Aden had sent out the sloop of war *Odin* under Leutnant Commander E. M. Palmer to search the approaches to the port. The Senior Officer was unsuspecting enough, he had merely wanted to check the efficacy of the Aden blackout, for there had been annoying reports that a good number of citizens were not dousing their lights in the evenings as required.

Lieutenant Commander Palmer was engaged in this dull but necessary task, when at just before four bells on the first dogwatch he spotted a shape about six miles off Aden harbour, and on going closer had seen it was a ship, heading on a westerly course at about eleven knots, and showing no lights. If she was a British ship, in these waters she should not be out prowling. If she was a neutral, she should be lit up like a teashop in the Strand on a rainy evening. It was all very suspicious and Palmer decided to find out just what was going on. He sent a blinker signal, in the clear, asking this stranger who she was and where she was going.

"*Turritella.* Supplies for troops carrying. Salonika heading am."

Certainly a most peculiar message, coming as it was from a British captain. Palmer's sense of smell was aroused.

"Stop immediately," went his second message. "I wish to board you."

"Why did not you stop me when I passed Aten," came the fretful reply. "Meadows. Master."

But Meadows, master of the *Turritella*, was not going to be spelling Aden, jewel of the British crown, in the German fashion, not if Leutnant Commander Palmer knew his British merchant captains. His suspicions were now complete and he began the chase in earnest, signalling his course and speed and position to all ships in the area.

The chase ran on into the morning watch, and for a time *Iltis* seemed to have a chance of getting away. Early on, the weather had been so fine that Palmer had been able to watch his quarry by the light of the moon, which was nearly full. At one bell on the morning watch, however, the moon set, and it grew very dark, so that Palmer lost sight of the other ship. He switched on his searchlights, scoured the sea, and there ahead, found *Iltis* and held her in the beam. It was a risky manoeuvre, for had she been *Wolf* with her seven big guns, those searchlight beams would have zeroed in the guns of Leutnant Witschetzky. But she was *Iltis*, armed only with a popgun on her poop, and she ran. Just before four bells on the morning watch, *Odin* came up fast, and Palmer made ready to lower a boat and board. Then the reason for the sudden changeabout was apparent, the boats of the other ship were in the water, and even as

Palmer watched, he heard two explosions, saw the quarry settle, and knew he had been right in his hunch. In half an hour the boats were picked up. They held the German and Chinese crew of *Turritella*, and the Chinese soon told all. They were, indeed, indifferent to the war of these European barbarians, and now *Wolf* and Brandes bore the brunt of it. The story of the capture of *Turritella* was told, and when the British broadcast the announcement about the raider in the Indian Ocean, they did not mean *Iltis* at all, but *Wolf* herself.

Nerger fretted nervously for a few days, waiting on the trade route for the reappearance of *Iltis*, which was supposed to rejoin him. The radio reports of the raider continued, and became more insistent, which aroused Nerger's suspicions that *Iltis* had fared badly. In that light, he must consider his own situation, and the dangers he ran in remaining long in this general position. The seaplane afforded him excellent protection, but only during the daylight hours, and only in clement weather when it could be lifted over the side and set bobbing in the sea. Captain Nerger felt uneasy, and that it was time to leave.

On Sunday 11 March, he had planned his usual weekly inspection. The men were washed and shaved and in their clean whites, and lining up ready for his attention, when the lookouts piped up.

"Smoke ho! Two points off the port bow."

The inspection was forgotten, the drums beat and the bells rang and the men went to action stations, prisoners who had been brought up for airing hustled down below to their hot, heavy compartment. *Wölfchen* was hastily put over the side and the pilot radioed back that he saw a cargo ship, about forty miles away, heading on the course *Wolf* was following.

The chase was not so easy. The steamer was fast, and after a time, when she was still a good way off, her captain seemed to sense that he was being followed and acted accordingly. At noon, the points of her mast appeared above the horizon, but it was four o'clock, well into the afternoon, before *Wolf* overhauled the merchantman and began the usual routine. The ship stopped. She had no choice as her captain knew, for he too had heard the messages about the presence of a raider in the Indian Ocean, and he knew what he was up against.

She was the English ship *Wordsworth*, of the Shakespeare line, carrying seven thousand tons of rice from Rangoon to London. It was a war cargo, very much so, and Captain Nerger felt a surge of pride in denying the British so much food, half a million pounds worth of cargo, plus the value of the ship. The prisoners were brought aboard, along with four hundred tons of very poor quality Indian coal, and the *Wordsworth* was consigned to Davy Jones.

Nerger now learned of the description given out by the Chinese of his ship and the seaplane, and this gave him serious pause. The British had swung into action, he could begin to feel it in his bones, and it was time to be moving away from this area. The German raider captain was quite right. On learning of the sinking of the *Iltis/Turritella*, the British Admiralty had stopped the movement of traffic into the Indian Ocean. All troopships at sea were met and escorted into Colombo. Then Admiral Wemyss in the East Indies and Admiral Charlton in South Africa were assigned to escort all troopships and supply freighters. Admiral Grant on the China station was warned about *Wolf* and advised to send his smaller ships out in divisions, rather than singly, lest they encounter this powerful German warship.

Two days before the capture of *Wordsworth*, the Admiralty reinforced the East Indies station with two cruisers, *Doris* and *Topaze*, and the old battleship *Exmouth*. Captain Nerger had reason to be proud: see how much British naval might he was tying up simply by his presence in this ocean. More Japanese vessels were brought into play, too, the *Tsushima* and *Niitaka* coming to Singapore. Yet at the moment, all these ships were not really so much occupied in searching for *Wolf* as in protecting the sheep of the merchant marine from her ravages. Convoy was the order of the day. It slowed delivery, and caused untold confusion and some hardship, but the convoy system at least meant *Wolf* would have trouble picking off strays. Convoy routes were established between Fremantle and Colombo, Fremantle and the Cape of Good Hope, Colombo and Bombay, and thence to the Persian Gulf. The Japanese government was asked to provide more force, and provided twenty-two ships. The British added to their forces until they had twenty-nine ships in this area. And all these ships were concentrating on one enemy, the *Wolf*. It was indeed time that Nerger moved his hunting grounds, lest he should be brought to bay. Time was on the side of his enemies, and it would take all his seamanship, courage, and foxiness to slip the traps that were being set for him.

6

Sunday Island

Three and a half months had elapsed since *Wolf* headed for the war, and in that short period she had consumed so much of her supply that the future looked bleak unless Captain Nerger was able to find coal and provisions very soon. Her captures had added captives—sixty more mouths to feed each day. Nerger had been told repeatedly by his captives that he would find no more coal on the Bombay-Aden run, for the ships had been taken off, rerouted, with the signs of raider trouble in the area. Now he believed them, and decided to head toward Australia, for he knew that what he needed must be found in these waters, and in the boundless Pacific he could also expect to find a haven in which to hole up for the refit his engineers were demanding. He ordered the course to be changed southward, and *Wolf* began to move south-southeast.

The crew knew that the ship was in trouble, for even the officers had fresh meat but once a week now, and the rest, prisoners, and enlisted men, ate dried vegetables, sea bread, and the tinned meat that on the lower deck was called "monkey meat." The potatoes had gone to eyes and rotted, the supply of pineapple and other delicacies "inherited" from the English was giving out. Everyone was ready for a change.

En route south, they encountered the sailing ship *Dee*, a three-masted bark in ballast, not much of a prize, but it was Nerger's task to blot from the sea all the English ships he could find, so he moved in to within six hundred yards, and hailed.

"Drehen Sie bei, ich schicke ein Boot," he announced through the megaphone and by signal. "Stand by, I am sending a boat."

The boarding crew discovered the ship was heading from Mauritius to West Australia. Not much of a haul. A white-haired captain who had spent twenty years at sea in this ship, Captain John B. Rugg, a French mate, and a dozen blacks as sailors. Very little of value, and more mouths to feed. Quickly the prisoners were brought aboard, and *Dee* was sunk so that *Wolf* might be on her way.

The course led ever southeast, through waters of increasing cold, seas of increasing strength, winds of increasing turbulence. By mid-April *Wolf* was well south of Tasmania and the cold was intense, a tremendous change from the steaming heat of the

Indian Ocean waters they had left. Rain, snow, clouds, heavy seas. Captain Nerger had headed into the Tasman Sea and toward New Zealand, hoping to intercept colliers on the run between the British colonies and South America. But he found nothing. The colliers were not using these black and forbidding waters.

Day after day the boring vigil grew harder to bear. The war news was very bad; British propagandists were predicting revolution in Germany and the overthrow of the Kaiser to stop the war, if the Kaiser did not die first, for he was reported to be mortally ill. Then came the news that the United States had declared war on Germany—more depressing news could hardly be found anywhere. Worst of all, nothing was stirring; there were no ships to be seen. From 17 April to 2 May, Captain Nerger cruised south of New Zealand, and then he gave it up disgustedly and headed into the Pacific. Two weeks off the rocky Stuart Islands had produced nothing at all, save chilblains.

The cold, the boredom, and the growing fear of the crew that no one would ever see the Fatherland again, were taking their tolls. Men fell sick, or thought they were sick, and crowded the sick bay. They complained about the food, and more about the lack of it. They clustered around the wireless room, which offered them the only diversion possible, and waited for word of the world outside. Morale sank to an all-time low. Captain Nerger was well aware of the problem. He skirted several island groups, looking for the haven where he would stop for repairs and some diversion. But none of these groups suited him, and he began zig-zagging northward, east of New Zealand, passing the international dateline and heading generally northward.

As they moved into more clement weather, the spirits of the crew revived a bit, until grief struck once more. This time it was fire in the coal hold. The second hold contained about a thousand tons of coal, which was most of what *Wolf* had left as reserve. Somehow, apparently through spontaneous combustion, it began to burn, early one Sunday morning. The watch sounded the alarm, the crew was roused, and the vital job of saving the ship began. White smoke filled the coal holds, half suffocating the men who moved in and out, coal sacks on their backs. Half a dozen men were sent to the sick bay with carbonic gas poisoning. For days the men went on fighting the fire.

His troubles so multiplied, Captain Nerger hastened to find his port of call, and settled finally on the Kermadec islands north of New Zealand. Specifically he was interested in Sunday Island. The charts and nautical journals showed that the Kermadecs were inhabited by the Bell family, but that their plantation had been deserted for a number of years. This place seemed ideal, for Sunday Island offered a protected harbour, where the ravages of the voyage to date could be repaired, and the fire fought more successfully.

In they went, to anchor. Immediately the engineers began tearing down the boilers, replacing parts, renewing rivets, working twenty-four hours a day in the black hole, while above the men of the upper decks manhandled coal hour after hour. Since *Wolf* was stationary, she did not even have the benefit of a breeze to blow away the dust, and so it settled everywhere, in the hammocks, in the crockery, in the men's lockers. The black gritty grime of coal became the central matter of existence.

It had been 22 May when they anchored on the southeast side of the island to begin the overhaul. A week later, enough work had been done below for the ship to get under way again, although she could only make about half speed until the work was finished. On the afternoon of 2 June, the lookouts who were ever-present aboard *Wolf* sang out:

"*Schiff in Sicht.*"

A ship—what ship? No matter, Captain Nerger was not happy. He was anything but ready for sea; to make steam would take time and he had no time. If this was a warship, he was in deep trouble. No matter what it was, it had to be dealt with, and immediately. There was only one thing to be done, and Nerger did it. He ordered the seaplane into the air, and Pilots Fabeck and Stein ran to do his bidding. The plane's engine began to crackle and then to roar, and in a few moments, Observer Stein was scouring the quiet surface of the lagoon, as they headed for the stranger.

Aboard this strange ship, the captain and officers of the cargo ship *Wairuna* were at lunch, when the plane began to move upward through the air. They knew there was a ship in harbour at Sunday Island, because Second Mate Rees had so informed the captain that morning when he caught sight of the masts of a large steamer on the other side of the high point called Mumukai, which protected the haven from the north. Rees had suggested the stranger might be a raider. Captain Saunders, who was new to the command, had scoffed at such old womanishness, and to exert his authority, here at the beginning of his voyage, had denied the mate's request to change course and skirt the islands.

Wireless Operator Roy Alexander could have been ordered to send a message back to New Zealand about a suspicious ship, and the Admiralty would have responded, for the whereabouts of the raider in the Indian Ocean were now totally unknown and a source of considerable puzzlement in Whitehall. But no such thing happened. The radio operator sat in his cabin, doing nothing. The *Wairuna* steamed past the headland, and the black steamer then came in view. Aboard *Wolf* the black gang was making steam, but it was a slow process, and Nerger knew he could never catch a fast enemy.

Pilot Fabeck flew in above the *Wairuna*, coming down very low, for he had a mission to perform, one given him by Captain Nerger in those hurried minutes before take-off. He came in masthigh, so low the men of *Wairuna* ducked involuntarily as the plane with its black maltese crosses passed overhead. Radioman Alexander ran to the bridge for orders, and he and Captain Saunders looked up to see an object falling from the plane onto the deck. The captain signalled the radioman to wait, while a seaman ran to pick up the object, a sandbag, with a message attached.

"Do not use your wireless," said the message. "Stop your engines. Put yourself under orders of the German auxiliary cruiser at Sunday Island or I will bomb you."

Ahead, Observer Stein was giving an indication of what he meant. He dropped a bomb in the sea just ahead of *Wairuna*, and it exploded, sending a gout of water into the air. The captain of *Wairuna* hesitated. He was steaming straight towards the enemy ship, he was threatened by a plane that he knew carried bombs. What was he to do? Perhaps Captain Saunders could have run for it. The seaplane might not have any more bombs, the raider might not be able to come out after him without a full head of steam, the gunners might miss as *Wairuna* fled. But Captain Saunders did not know that all these things could be true, and so he decided to surrender. He went below, and began burning papers, and told the wireless operator to destroy his log, and the radio set, and above all not to use the wireless key under any conditions.

Soon Leutnant Rose appeared with the landing and boarding party, and asked for the ship's papers. He learned that the ship was heading from Auckland to England via the Panama Canal, and that she had 1,500 tons of coal aboard. Soon the *Wairuna* was brought into the harbour to lay alongside *Wolf*, while the coal and usable supplies were transferred to the raider.

The *Wairuna* was captured on a Saturday. On Sunday not much was done, but on Monday the work began. It was hard work, for while the first few days of *Wolf's* stay here had seen such mild weather that shore parties were out every day, hunting wild goats and pigs, and fishing, and picking the oranges left on the trees grown by the Bell family, now the weather turned foul. On the second day the hawsers holding the ships together snapped suddenly in the swell, and it was another day before they could be brought together. The coaling was resumed, the cables snapped, and it all had to be done over again. There was more than coal: *Wairuna* was carrying a full consignment of stores, just a few hours out from home port, and she had forty sheep aboard—fresh meat for the crew.

When the weather was clement, Captain Nerger let Captain Meadows, the senior POW officer, take parties out fishing, and they caught enough big fish to supply the tables of officers, men and prisoners of the raider. They were odd fish, huge, some of them like snapper, some like huge bream, but striped yellow and black. Sometimes their catches were taken off the hook by sharks, but there was enough for all, and Nerger was so impressed by the sharks that he had the tail cut off one of them and hung on the bow of *Wolf* for good luck.

The stripping of *Wairuna* occupied two weeks, largely because of the vagaries of the weather, and then she was ready for sinking. A delay was brought when a sailing ship came barely into sight off to the northeast, but the ship tacked away without sighting or at least paying any attention to the two steamers in the little harbour, and so the following day, Captain Nerger took raider and captive out to sea, two miles from the island, and then used *Wairuna* for gunnery practice, not because he wanted to, but because the time bombs set in the engine room failed to detonate, and he did not want to send a crew back aboard. So the shells poured into *Wairuna*, smashing into the engine room, tearing holes in her steel sides, and finally bringing her to heel and to turn slowly over to port, her funnel snapping off as she lay on her side, the cargo hatches bursting with the pressure, and hides and wool bales coming out to bob on the sea until they grew water-logged and sank.

That was the end of *Wairuna*, almost at the beginning of her voyage. And because Captain Nerger had decided to keep his captives aboard the raider, and because cargo ships were very quiet and self-contained during these war days, it would be months before anyone really missed her.

The days of quiet in the island harbour were now ended for the crew of *Wolf*. She was ready for sea again, ready to go a-raiding. There were some shortages: the seaplane needed fuel; the furnaces needed new brickfire, but *Wolf* would get along.

Hardly had *Wolf* left the Kermadecs when a sail came in sight, and as the seaplane circled and identified the vessel, Captain Nerger smiled broadly. *Winslow*, she was, sailing from Sidney to Apia. No more need be said, for Nerger knew all about this ship and had for a month. Listening in to the area radio traffic during those dull weeks when nothing was happening, the men of *Wolf* had heard that the people of Samoa were crying out for supplies. They needed coal, firebricks, petrol, medical supplies, and they had no ships to go and get them. Sydney and Auckland had first protested that they could not supply any ships, but then they had promised that a relief vessel would be sent and they named her: the *Winslow*. Nerger had looked her up in Lloyd's register, a little sailing schooner not worth fooling with under normal conditions. But now, seeing her, knowing her cargo, he decided to take her, and did so in very short order. Here on a silver platter was the fuel for the aeroplane, the firebrick, and even more coal, although 350 tons would not take them far. Also, and not at all to be sneezed at, eighteen hams.

So the four-masted sailing ship was hailed, and then brought alongside, and finally taken back into the Sunday Island anchorage to unload the precious supplies. The unloading went on day and night until it was finished, for Captain Nerger was eager to be about his Emperor's business. Then *Winslow* was sailed out into open water by the German prize crew. Charges did not bring her down, and Leutnant Witschetzky's gun crews had to do the job. They holed the wooden sailing vessel time after time but being wooden and stubborn, she continued to float. They waited, for she must be destroyed, and finally, hours later, she did go down. Then *Wolf* moved away, her captain knowing precisely what he was going to do next: he was going into the waters around New Zealand, to lay mines on the routes that connected this colony with Australia.

The date was 22 June. The relative inactivity of the past month had led the British to relax their defences once again, and besides this, the search for *Wolf* was centred on the Indian Ocean and the Cape Route, not the far reaches of the Pacific. The past five days had been spent stripping the *Winslow*, but every man, down to the prisoners, knew that *Wolf* was ready to go a-raiding once again. The prisoners, during this period, had been given unusal freedom; they were allowed to go ashore on parties with German guards, to go fishing in the shark-filled waters for the big fish; to stay on the poop deck of the *Wolf* most of the day

72

if they wished, as long as they did not make any trouble. After all, where were they to go?

On 22 June, just after disposing of the *Winslow*, Captain Nerger learned where some thought they might go. Chief Officer Steers and Second Engineer Clelland from the *Turritella* had disappeared. They had gone over the side late on the evening of 21 June, hung from the rudder until dark, and then swum for the shore of Sunday Island, a mile away. Captain Meadows and the others had wished them Godspeed, and better, had answered to their names in the informal roll calls that marked this period of captivity. Nerger had had no report of the missing men until next day when the ship was far from Sunday Island—too far to trouble to go back and undertake a costly and perhaps impossible search for the escaped prisoners. It seemed unlikely that Steers and Clelland would be found anyhow for many months, because literally no one stopped at Sunday Island these days, so Nerger was not as dismayed as he might have been. Indeed, as it turned out, he need not have been dismayed at all, for Steers and Clelland were never seen again. They either drowned, or were eaten by sharks, or lost their lives in the mountain jungle of the island before any other vessel ever visited there.

Yet the precedent was so serious that Nerger had to take strong action to control his prisoners. He did not yet know it, but Captain Meadows had been secreting bottles in the prisoners' quarters; whenever he felt that there was a chance a current might carry a bottle to some civilized place, he threw one overboard, carefully sealed to protect a message that gave all possible information about

Wolf so that the British cruisers might find and destroy her. The discovery of the missing prisoners, made by Leutnant von Oswald, brought an order that the prisoners be kept in their quarters and not allowed on deck for the next month. If the move was to break their morale, it did anything but; the men of the captured ships were quite pleased that they had so put out their enemy, and hoped that Steers and Clelland would get away to tell the whole story.

Wolf now moved into the Tasman Sea, literally into the heart of the enemy's waters, where she could expect to see none but British warships. In the hold Captain Meadows was cheered, and offered to bet anyone that in the next two weeks they would all be captured and that would be the end of *Wolf*. In his cabin Nerger was cheered, because he had taken a little time to read the newspapers captured from *Winslow* and learned that the ships *Perseus* and *Worcestershire* and *City of Paris* had gone down to his mines off Colombo, that the troop transport *Tyndarus* had hit one of the mines off Cape Agulhas, and although it had not gone down it had been delayed and the troops had to be taken off, that the steamer *Celitia* had also hit a mine off the cape. So far, the cruise was eminently satisfactory.

As *Wolf* steamed along, the mines were brought up on deck and the navigator made for Cape Maria van Diemen, the northernmost point of New Zealand, and the cape the British called North Cape. She stood well off land, this comfortable merchant ship, nosing gently into the swell, until night fell and she headed inward to lay her minefield. The clamp was down on the prisoners:

the punishment for helping escapees was part of it, but they were not even allowed to go to the latrines up under the poop deck; the steel hatch cover was down and dogged.

The minelaying equipment had been stowed during the days after the Bombay raid, so now the steel rails had to be reset, leading to their two openings in the stern. The mines were run down the length of the deck on little carriages, and then slid over to drop into the sea behind the ship, each offering the enemy 350 pounds of explosive, set to go off at about fifteen feet below the surface, so that fishermen and small vessels would not be bothered but the big ships would become the prey. The Sunday Island interlude was far behind them now, and the men of *Wolf* were back at their task of destruction.

7

None but the Enemy

The night of 25 June 1917 was black and thick off the North Cape of New Zealand, the rain squalls pelting the ship every fifteen minutes or so and making it very hard for any watchers anywhere to see. Captain Nerger was delighted; he could not have asked for better weather for the task at hand. He waited until four bells in the second dog watch, and then began moving in towards shore. One last task had to be performed to prepare for the minelaying, and this was done: the stern rails of the ship were removed, the mining doors opened, and the track along the deck extended out well beyond the stern so as to minimize any danger to the propellers from a faulty mine that might explode on dropping.

The mines were laid on the track, one by one, and trundled along to the end, and then began plopping into the water, dropped in groups of five. *Wolf* would drop five mines, then zig-zag, and twenty minutes later drop some more. The area between the North Cape, Cape Maria van Diemen and the rocks northward known as the Three Kings was well covered. Below, the prisoners dropped off to sleep, except for Second Mate Rees of the *Wairuna*, he who had warned his captain that the masts over the edge of the rock of Sunday Island might be a raider, only to be put down harshly. Rees was fighting his war that night, taking careful note of the track of the ship as well as he could, and the number of mines laid. He would keep count of the track and the mines all the way along, hoping to find some way to give this information to the British authorities and help bring an early end to Captain Nerger's so far successful career. Before dawn, all mines were laid, and the field was as Nerger wanted it to be, not large—perhaps twenty-five mines in all—but adequate to arouse the enemy again and bring numbers of protective vessels to cover these waters long after *Wolf* had steamed away.

Nerger headed now for the south, steaming down the west coast of New Zealand's north island. He was not overly pleased with the performance of the ship, even after the home-made refit at Sunday Island. She would make just over ten knots, for her hull was foul and she needed the services of a drydock.

There seemed little chance of her having any

78

such help; the ship was surrounded by enemies, with only the Dutch showing a determined neutrality in all the Pacific. Just now, on 27 June, she was off New Plymouth, the snow-topped peak of Mount Egmont standing above, heading for Cape Egmont and the Cook Strait. It was midwinter in these waters, and quite cold, but the water around the cape, which could be very nasty, was this day absolutely calm.

Again the ship was rigged for minelaying, and this time forty-five mines were laid in the narrow strait that separates the two main islands of New Zealand. Then Nerger headed west, toward the Australian coast, where the captain of the raider intended to lay a minefield on the route followed by steamers plying between Melbourne and Sydney.

There was a good deal of radio traffic concerning *Wolf* on the airwaves that day, for the minefield off Bombay had just claimed the *Mongolia*, and the story of *Wolf* was out, courtesy of the Chinese sailors of *Turritella*. But the talk was about the Indian Ocean, while *Wolf* was here in the shadow of Australia. So far no one had missed *Wairuna* or *Winslow* and there was no way of connecting them with *Wolf*. Nerger did worry a little about those two prisoners who had presumably escaped to Sunday Island, but there was nothing to be done about that.

Wolf's disguise as a merchantman came in handy this day, for on the coast of Australia they sighted any number of other ships, made careful moves to avoid coming too close, and played the part of the innocent black cargo vessel to a T.

Nerger had relaxed the iron discipline imposed

on the prisoners after leaving Cape Farewell on the morning of 26 June, but every time a plume of smoke appeared on the horizon, the bells clanged, the men of *Wolf* went to action stations, and the prisoners went down their hatch. When the raider *Emden* had perused the southern waters two years before, Captain von Müller had called his men to action with the traditional bugle, but the bugle was never used aboard *Wolf*. It would have marked her as a warship, so the bells and buzzers did the job instead.

The ship headed nervously for Gabo light, the lookouts alert, the radiomen listening anxiously to the transmission of the shore bases, and the military ships at sea—all their enemies. Every man spent most of his time at his action station, consequently crew and prisoners lived on black bread and coffee for the most part during the six days of the crossing, until they reached the point Nerger wanted off New South Wales.

At night on the sixth day the minelaying preparations began again. Darkness fell, and around two bells of the second dogwatch the ship began to speed up, on the route between Cape Howe and Gabo light. The minelaying began, the ship following the old zig-zag pattern, but this night at top speed, as though Nerger knew full well the danger he was in, and was eager to be out of it and away.

Perhaps half the mines he intended were laid, another twenty-five, when the lookouts sighted a smoke plume, and then the tell-tale tall masts of a British cruiser. She was the *Encounter* (although Nerger did not know it at that moment) and she was out looking for trouble. Nerger sounded the call to battle stations, the guns were run out (there was no chance for concealment of activity while the mine track was in full view astern and the mines were all on deck—and he waited nervously. The darkness of night gave him one chance: he could slip away, without being silhouetted by the moon or the light at Gabo, if he were quick enough. So *Wolf* stopped all else, and changed course, briskly trying to preserve an air of innocence. *Encounter* slid by on the horizon seeing nothing out of the ordinary, and the moment of grave danger was past. *Wolf* was not so foolhardy as to try to run back in and finish the job. She made out into the Tasman sea seeking broad water for safety.

As *Wolf* headed for the southern waters of New Zealand once again, the mines were returned to their compartment, and the crew waited for the new indications of activity the captain would pursue. First thing was to change her looks, and the crew went to work, cutting down the funnel, chopping off the tops of the masts, changing her lines and her colours. Then, warned by some instinct, Captain Nerger decided to head north instead of south, and turned the ship around and headed up the Tasman Sea for the open Pacific.

Nerger's hunch was almost immediately confirmed. He had gone south for two days after the minelaying off the Australian coast, and that made it 5 July when he made the change in course. On that day, the Steamer *Cumberland* sailed out from Sydney for England, via South Africa, a big nine thousand ton cargo ship of the Federal Steam Navigation Company, carrying a cargo of frozen meat for England's war effort.

81

The night was fine, the ship responded to her helm in the quiet sea, and the voyage seemed destined to be a happy one. Then, just before midnight on 6 July, *Cumberland*'s happy voyage ended, her plates were stove in by a giant explosion, and she began taking water heavily. Her captain headed in toward the shore and beached her to save her from sinking.

When the navy arrived, the captain of *Cumberland* stated flatly that he had either been torpedoed or had struck a mine. Torpedoed? Nonsense, said the navy. There were no German submarines within ten thousand miles. A mine? Equal nonsense. The captain ought to know that His Majesty's navy did not leave loose mines lying about, and as for a German minelayer, well, obviously it was out of the question. No, said the navy, the captain had obviously been the victim of "internal explosions" of some variety, and the implication was very clear that the explosions must have been the captain's own fault. Equal nonsense, shouted the Australian press. The internal explosions must have been caused by the revolutionaries of the IWW, the International Workers of the World, those "Wobblies" who were using the war effort to further their vile designs.

So over this affair, Australia erupted into violent political battle. The case of the mine and the *Cumberland* was almost forgotten, the presence of *Wolf* in these waters was never even suspected, and ships began to disappear. The collier *Undola* just dropped out of sight, and no one ever discovered what happened to her. Mines came ashore within the sight of watchers and smashed on the beach. A group of natives of New Zealand found a

82

mine, and tried to haul it back to their camp. There was an explosion, those Maoris were never seen again, and a large hole was left in the beach.

Finally, the authorities began to think there might just possibly have been a minelayer at work in New Zealand-Australian waters, but by this time, *Wolf* was long, long gone. Even so, the authorities were right to be concerned, because passenger steamer *Wimmera* struck one of *Wolf*'s mines off the Three Kings in the summer of 1918, a year after they were laid, and went down very quickly, with the loss of some thirty lives.

When the hunt began in seriousness for the raider in the Pacific, the Japanese put to sea a squadron of twenty-six vessels to aid in the search. Captain Nerger sensed this as he changed his course and headed north, and he also hoped to find a vessel with a good supply of coal, for the fuel taken from *Wairuna* was going fast. Six days out of Gabo, the weather had turned fine, for the ship left the southernmost latitudes and was entering the Pacific, in clear, shining days, and cool but not cold nights. Nerger sought the Sydney-Suva sea lane, hoping here to find victims.

He found one the very first day, in the middle of the afternoon. A lookout sighted a sail, and the raider made chase and caught up with her in an hour. The boarding party cast off and moved across the water in the ship's pinnace. Leutnant Rose had just clambered up the ladder and was questioning the captain of this American three-masted bark, when a lookout shouted.

"Ship in sight!"

Captain Nerger lifted his glasses. There on the skyline was one of the biggest, blackest smoke smudges he had ever seen, and it was heading direct for *Wolf*.

Was this a trap laid by the British enemy for the unsuspecting raider? It certainly could be, it would be the most sensible thing in the world for the enemy to bait the water with an old sailing ship, which would seem easy prey, and then lurk just beyond the horizon, and sweep down on the raider as she was making the kill.

There was no time to linger. Captain Nerger sent a quick signal to the boarding party, telling them to sail the bark to a point sixty miles southeast of their present position, and wait there for him. Then he ordered full steam ahead, and turned away from the gathering smoke on the horizon; there was absolutely no time to lose if he was to escape with his ship making ten knots to what would be the eighteen of a shiny British cruiser.

But either *Wolf* was too canny, or the other ship had another mission, Nerger decided, because in an hour they were safely over the horizon, the smoke had disappeared, and when the plane was sent aloft to discover what it might, pilot Fabeck reported absolutely nothing in sight.

Captain Nerger was very careful. He lurked in the area that night, and at dawn sent the seaplane up again for a look. Still nothing. So the plane was recovered, and the course set for the rendez-vous point. When still well off, the seaplane was launched again, and this time she circled the sailing ship, to make sure that all was well. Stein reported back that there was no sign of any other ship around the sailor, that he had flown low over her and the prize crew had waved gaily at him, and that all seemed very well indeed. Nerger was satisfied, he headed up to the bark, and briskly took over.

Leutnant Rose came aboard *Wolf* with news that was interesting, and some of it a little disturbing. First, the ship was the American bark *Beluga*, bound from San Francisco to Sydney with a cargo of benzine. That meant a supply of fuel for the seaplane that would last many months. Second, Rose reported, the ship carried a woman, the captain's wife, and a little child, their six-year-old daughter Anita.

A woman and child aboard the raider? What would be done with them? Mrs. Cameron, the captain's wife, worried about that more than Nerger, but there was no need. The German captain assigned the family a cabin amidships, booting one of the officers out to live with a brother for a time. He also informed Mrs. Cameron that they would be moved off the ship and sent homeward at the very first opportunity. *Wolf* was a German warship, and Nerger's treatment of this American captain and his family was more than punctilious; the only restriction on the American captain was that he should stay in the cabin when requested, and make no attempt to contact the other prisoners.

Wolf then went back to work. First *Beluga* was destroyed that same day, shells from the guns setting afire her benzine cargo. The shells whistled in, smashing into the wooden sides that had seemed so sound and now seemed so frail. The benzine spilled out into the sea, flaming, high as the masts, and spreading out into the sea until the sailing ship seemed to move in an ocean of fire. The blaze was so bright that *Wolf* headed off, not

waiting for the ship to sink, because the fire
would certainly attract any vessel anywhere in the
vicinity. But within a matter of hours, *Wolf* was
back on the sealane which seemed so promising, at
26°S, 166° E, looking for victims.

A month had now passed since an angry captain
Nerger had imposed punishment on the prisoners,
and he relaxed the restrictions. They began to
come above decks for an hour or two a day, and
were even allowed to watch the operations of
Wölfchen, the *Wolf's* cub, that protected the
mother ship and hunted for her. Morning and evening, the two-seater seaplane was hoist by cargo
derrick from its resting place atop the Number
Three hatch on the after deck, and over the side.
Usually both Fabeck and Stein went up, one flying, the other acting as observer. It was dull work
for the most part, for day after day went by without the stir of anything on the horizon larger than
an albatross. Nerger considered moving on, but his
fuel and food situations were growing very serious, and he thought it would be best to wait on
this lane, using as little fuel as possible, until a
freighter or passenger steamer came along. So
they waited, with some impatience. For prisoners
and sailors, the routine was much the same. The
call to turn to came just after daylight, and the
men crowded to the heads to wash—each man re-
ceiving one dipper of water for the task. If a
sailor or a prisoner needed to wash clothes, he
made deals with others to save the wash water until he had enough. For water, like food was ra-
tioned these days. Shortly after dawn, the
seaplane took off for its hour's morning flight.
Then it was recovered, and by the beginning of

the day watch it was time for breakfast, which consisted of black bread and coffee.

The men of *Wolf* had already turned to on the pumps, hosing down the decks with sea water and getting the ship right for the day. They set to work on their daily tasks, checking ammunition, cleaning the guns, painting—all the things that keep a ship healthy on a long cruise. The prisoners lounged about, either watching, or playing cards, or reading. Much of the time was whiled away yarning, either sea stories, or more likely tall tales of adventures with wine, women, and song in far-off ports. The supply of tinned corned beef was running out and everyone aboard the raider now began to eat strange exotic dishes. *Turritella*'s rice and *Wordsworth*'s rice and cinnamon comprised the basic ration. The cooks had scratched their heads about what to do with a cargo of prunes found aboard *Beluga*, and ended up by making soup of them, combining prunes, bully beef and rice into a sweet but not sickening dish that was served nearly every day. That came at noon, the big meal, which was followed in the day's routine by change of watch for the Germans and the dull routine of prison life for the captives.

On weekdays, the evening meal came at five o'clock, and consisted of black bread and coffee again. On Sundays the routine changed; there was church service in the morning; a better meal at midday; and a concert by the ship's band, which the captives swore was the worst German band in the history of music. The reason, one German officer once confided to a British counterpart, was that the men who played the horns had been chosen as seamen and fighters, not as musicians, as

87

was the usual practice of all navies. So they played their tubas and cornets as though they were firing the 6 inch guns, and the result was a noise almost as frightening.

When captives were first taken on board, they all had accepted the command system under which Captain Meadows was in charge, as senior officer present. But as time went on, the prison hold filled with men of many nationalities, and many walks of life. When the *Wairuna* was taken, the captain managed to save his most precious possession, a favourite armchair—and this bit of furniture nearly caused a revolution aboard *Wolf*. For the first few weeks, Captain Saunders had undisputed possession of his chair. Then one day he came to his part of the quarters to find a young steward lolling in it, and the steward refused to get out, claiming that they were all prisoners and thus were all equal. Men loyal to the captain jumped the steward, knocked him out of the chair, and about the deck a bit, and the commotion brought Leutnant von Oswald, the prison officer of the ship, who sternly told the steward he would be shot if he attempted any more insubordination.

But the results were not quite so tidy. The Germans decided to separate senior officers, putting them in the after port corner of the compartment, from junior officers in the forward port corner and the ordinary seamen or ratings, on the whole starboard side. Thus a caste system was established, which set up conflicts among the prisoners. It also set up another problem, because to enforce the segregation the Germans sent down packing crates, which were fashioned into living

88

quarters and lockers, and then provided a marvellous haven for lice. Within a matter of two weeks the lice infestation grew so serious the German medical officers had to come down and delouse the prisoners regularly.

The routine was the same, day after day, as July wore on. On the fourteenth of the month there was a slight diversion from plan. Pilots Fabeck and Stein went aloft as usual, and got up to around two thousand feet on the great circle they flew around *Wolf*, when the plane's engine begin to miss. Fabeck was at the controls, and he glided down, trying to get alongside his ship before being forced into the sea. The glide was smooth and flat, until the plane came to a point about a mile from the ship, still at around two hundred feet. Then the seaplane was snatched by a downdraught, dropped suddenly, and smacked into the sea with such force that the two floats were destroyed and broken off, and one wing crumpled. The nose went under, the tail came up, and the two pilots scrambled up onto the tail and waited anxiously as *Wolf* sped toward them to save the plane before it sank.

The ship's boats scurried to the side of the beleaguered *Wölfchen*, fastened lines to keep it from sinking, and the cargo derrick moved the sad wrecked plane back aboard the ship. But it was so badly smashed that the prisoners bet (they would bet on anything) that the plane could never be rebuilt. The carpenters set to work, trying to rebuild the smashed wing and pontoons from materials aboard the ship, but Captain Nerger had very little hope that they would be able to restore the eyes of the *Wolf*.

As if to counterbalance this disaster, fate next day sent *Wolf* a present, in the form of another sail. The ship was quickly overhauled, and proved to be the American schooner *Encore* carrying a cargo of timber from Portland, Oregon to Sydney. Far more useful to the Germans was the food of the *Encore*, case after case of American canned fruits and vegetables, with lots of pickles and spices and sauces to help break the monotony of rice and cinnamon and prune soup. *Encore* was taken off the rock called Hunter Island, at 21° S, 16° E, very close to Fiji. Following a hunch again, Captain Nerger moved swiftly away from this route. The coal situation was becoming very nearly desperate, and Nerger now had to make a most difficult decision. If he stayed on the major trade routes, he had to move at top speed in order to avoid the danger of being trapped by a British cruiser. If he moved to less heavily patrolled waters, he ran the danger of never finding a ship to capture, of eventually running out of coal altogether, and then living out what was left of life floating hopelessly in the endless ocean, perhaps even praying for capture in the hot sun. He bit the bullet and decided to take the latter course. It would last longer at any rate. So he headed north and then northwest, keeping clear of the New Hebrides, and slowing to about four knots, which meant a drastic cut in the curve of fuel consumption.

The prisoners were having more troubles than ever and the capture of *Beluga* emphasized them. She was an American ship, with an American captain, a big Swede named Olsen, but many of her crew were Scandinavians who had not obtained their final American papers. Nerger, who could always use extra hands, offered the Scandinavians the freedom of the ship, as neutrals, if they would help in the stripping of captures, which would free his fighting men to do their jobs. Half the crew of *Beluga* went with the Germans, and so did some other neutrals from other ships, much to the disgust of the British and Americans in the prison hold. There was bad blood now, and the prisoners spent as much time hating one another as they did hating the Germans.

The *Wolf* steamed slowly toward the Solomon Islands, the men sweating heavily in the heat, the prisoners stripping down to a pair of shorts and a singlet. All the while the carpenters hammered at their work to build the floats and wing. All the while, Captain Nerger worried over his next course of action. He gave very serious consideration to pulling in at Tulagi, the capital of the Solomons, and holding up the Australian and New Zealand merchants there for their supply of coal. The very thought shows Nerger's desperation, for it was well known that Tulagi had an excellent wireless—the radiomen heard it every night, and to stop there would be to commit suicide. The British would immediately begin scouring the South Pacific, and *Wolf*'s chance of ever getting home would be reduced to minuscule. Captain Nerger hung about the area as long as he dared, hoping to intercept the monthly supply steamer from Sydney, but he had no such luck. Finally he realized that bold action was his only salvation, and he decided on a run to New Guinea. There at least, he would deliver more of his deadly mines, and as for the future, then he would see.

And as he made that decision, fate again threw

the dice for him. On the radio one night came a message: the supply steamer *Matunga* was about to set forth for her monthly trip to New Guinea. The wireless station gave Rabaul full details for the eager people: the cargo, the route, the departure date, the estimated time of arrival. All Nerger had to do now was navigate, and his problems were going to be solved.

8

The Third Phase

In the beginning, Captain Nerger had set out from Germany with the admiralty's orders to go to the Indian Ocean, lay mines, and raid. First he had laid his mines, then he had raided, but the results had not been as spectacular as he had hoped. He was generally satisfied, for he had caused a good deal of havoc among the British enemy, but the very caution that led him to keep his prisoners and avoid any publicity about his whereabouts, also tended to minimize the search for him. Now, with his new decision, Nerger knew full well that he would become the object of one of the greatest sea hunts of all time. He would take *Matunga*, but almost immediately the hunt would be on for him.

So he must act boldly, and make no mistakes from this point on, if he and the crew of *Wolf* were ever to see Germany.

In the last days of July, the work was finished on the seaplane, and the floats were tested and found seaworthy. The wing was a different matter: the only way to test it was to try to fly the airplane. If it flew, good; if it crashed, too bad. Pilots Fabeck and Stein were the ones to worry about that. Gingerly, on the morning of 29 July, they took to the air. It flew. All was well. *Wolf* was now ready to eat up the Sydney-Rabaul mail steamer.

The affair seemed ridiculously simple. On 27 July the steamer *Matunga* had left Sydney for Brisbane and Rabaul, telling all the world by radio messages in the clear. She was taking a cargo of supplies, including a good deal of coal, passengers, and troops to garrison the new British colony. Yes, New Guinea was a new British colony then; it had been seized from Germany at the beginning of the war, and Australia was administering the islands of New Guinea, New Britain, and New Ireland. Among the passengers was Colonel Strangman, acting administrator of the new colony, and his twenty troops were escorting him back to Rabaul. Captain A. Donaldson of the *Matunga* managed a crew of forty-five, which was quite adequate to handle the middle-aged single crew steamer of 1,600 tons. She was not beautiful, but she was roomy and seaworthy and she did her job, which was not very glamorous either.

Just as the *Wolf* cub returned from its flight on the morning of 29 July, and the pilots marched to the bridge to report to Captain Nerger, their conversation was interrupted by the wireless officer, carrying a handful of messages. Nerger told him to report, and the officer read out the message interchanges between Herrnsheim and Co. and Wahlen and Co. of New Guinea, and their representatives in Australia. Ironically, the two New Guinea firms were solid German enterprises, still run by the German owners under the new government—and they were the cause of all the excitement aboard *Wolf*, quite unknowingly presenting Nerger with vital information. The messages described the cargo (five hundred tons of lovely hard coal among other things) and the voyage. Captain Donaldson announced that this very day, 29 July, he was sailing from Brisbane and would arrive at Rabaul on 7 August. He had "the coal for Burrows" he said, and the cargo of beer for one of the Rabaul firms.

Nerger strode to the chart table, and looked down at the New Guinea area. If Donaldson planned to be in Rabaul on the seventh, that meant he would have to pass through St. George's Channel on the fifth, and that would be a very nice place to lie in wait for him. He gave the orders, the ship's course was changed and the engines stepped up the tempo of their hum, as *Wolf* moved purposefully northward to intercept the steamer. Morning and evening the seaplane flew, for rather than growing overconfident, Captain Nerger was being more cautious than usual, and warned the pilots to keep alert for any ship at all. He knew the Japanese cruiser *Chikuma* was in these waters at the moment, and he had no desire to encounter her. He also knew now that *Matunga* had a radio, and it was imperative that he get close enough to the ship without being observed for what he was, so that if any attempt was made to send a message, *Wolf*'s guns could wreck the island steamer's radio room very quickly. Speed was very important, for in the South Pacific radio played a vital part in the life of the colonists, and there were at least two stations close by that would be alert and would immediately transmit to the world any signs of trouble they might get from *Matunga*.

There was another point. The radio traffic also indicated that the island steamer *Morinda* would be returning from its mail run to Sydney at this time. The *Morinda* would have delivered all its western supplies to the islands it served, and would be full of copra, which was of no use to *Wolf*. This venture against *Matunga* was not just a raid against British shipping, but an essential capture for the life of *Wolf*. If she did not have coal and supplies she was almost finished right here in these warm Pacific waters.

On the fifth, *Wolf* reached a point about midway between the Solomons and Huon Gulf in New Guinea, some 275 miles from Rabaul. Late in the afternoon Fabeck and Stein took off, and were gone an hour and a half, without sending any signal. The plane buzzed over New Guinea itself, and was spotted there by plantation workers, but that brought no trouble because the plantations were still German and the owners were not in close communication with the British authority. They had seen nothing, said Stein ruefully, as he reported to the bridge. No sign of a ship within a hundred miles. Stein had just clicked his heels and was leaving the bridge, when the wireless officer appeared again, very excited. *Matunga* had just radioed Rabaul her position, course, and time of arrival. A few moments at the charts, and Stein and Fabeck were back over the side again in *Wölfchen*, warming up the engine and making ready for one more flight. This was a very dangerous undertaking; the little seaplane was now put together with baling wire, so to speak, and it was certain that by the time they finished their flight the sudden darkness of the tropics would have descended. They took off knowing that they were going to have to make a night landing when they came back, and the thought was not comforting.

The plane circled and headed in the direction Captain Nerger had indicated. The drone was soon lost in the gathering sunset, and darkness enmantled the dark ship. The prisoners were allowed late on deck—it was Nerger's habit to let them see most of the activity of the plane and captures, not because he wanted to impress them, but because he knew the amusement value of any sort of break in the routine, and he wanted to avoid trouble with his growing prison camp. So the prisoners were out on deck, lounging and gossiping, and they saw the white and red rockets from the Very pistol Stein fired by prearranged signal to tell Nerger what he wanted to know about the *Matunga*. The sound of the plane's engine grew louder as it circled back to find the mother ship in the darkness; Nerger lit up for the cub, and suddenly the noise level changed, the plane swooped down, and landed splashing in the water alongside *Wolf*, and taxied up to the derrick as saucily as if it were noon.

Two hours later, the lights of the *Matunga* appeared to the south, and the blacked-out *Wolf* now closed stealthily on the unsuspecting passenger freighter. Just before daylight, Nerger dropped back. When the sun came up, he launched the seaplane again, with orders to get out of the area and stay out until after the action was over. The plane had to be kept in full sight on top of the Number Three hatch, or disassembled and hidden. Since it took a couple of hours to take it apart and the same to put it together again, it was scarcely a good idea to knock down *Wölfchen* right now, but it was not a good idea to leave it on deck because the sight of it would send the wind up with the *Matunga*, and that radio was too dangerous to leave unsettled even for a few moments. All the mysteries of *Wolf*'s disguise must now be brought into play.

The men were warned to conceal themselves with even more care than usual. The guns were manned, the torpedo tubes ready; every sailor was at his action station, as the *Wolf* moved sloppily, it seemed, across the course of the smaller ship. The raider created a commotion, of course, but only because she was a big cargo ship where few such were usually seen, and on the decks of *Matunga* people were speculating about her ownership and her destination. It did not occur to anyone that she might be a German raider, for as all the world knew Australian waters were completely safe from raiders. Nerger tried to give the impression that he was coming close out of sheer neighbourliness, to have a hail and a few words with a friendly captain. Then, when a few hundred yards only separated the two vessels, the false plates swung away, the guns of *Wolf* were re-

98

vealed in all their narrow grisliness, and the warning shot of the sea boomed out to splash across the bow of *Matunga*, as *Wolf* ran up the unmistakable battle flag of the German navy and the signal flags with their message to stop and be boarded.

Matunga complied without a whimper. Captain Donaldson told the wireless operator to shut down his rig, and on the bridge the officers waited for the boarding party to come across the narrowing gap of water in the pinnace. Leutnant Rose was all smiles as he stepped aboard the *Matunga* and marched to the bridge.

"Good morning, Mr. Donaldson," he said, giving a little bow. Captain Donaldson's jaw dropped. How did this German know his name? It all seemed very mysterious. Rose was very businesslike. He informed the captain that he had been captured, delivered the German war flag to the seaman who moved to pull down the Union Jack and put up the red white and black ensign. Rose then put his own quartermaster at the wheel, and sent his own engineer down to the boilers, and delivered concise orders that put *Matunga* in line behind *Wolf*, following her new leader.

As they departed, the officials aboard *Matunga* were moved by boat over to *Wolf*. Colonel Strangman had with him two majors, a captain, as well as a doctor, who had his wife with him, the soldiers, a maid who belonged to one of the houses in Rabaul, and a dozen planters. The Australian Captain McIntosh was well acquainted with relations of Leutnant Witschetzky in Sydney, and they had a good chat about these mutual connections, as the officials and Captain Donaldson were interrogated by Captain Nerger and his officers.

Meanwhile, the ships steamed north for two days, swinging west past Kavieng on New Ireland, to approach the coast of New Guinea at a virtually deserted point. As they moved, Rose and his prize crew examined at leisure what they had caught for their captain. There was the coal, invaluable. There was the beer, hundreds of cases of it, forty-eight bottle cases—enough to last *Wolf*'s crew for all the rest of their voyage. There was also liquor, cases and cases and cases of whisky and gin and other spirits, the month's supply for all Rabaul's colonials, the club and the whole works. There were also tobaccos and cigarettes by the carton, chocolate and other sweets, fresh vegetables and canned fruits, and dozens of newspapers and magazines that told the officers a good deal about life in England and Australia and something about the war.

Captain Donaldson was a South Pacific sailor who had been on the run a long while, and had developed his own way of life very satisfactorily. He came to the bridge and asked to send a message to his company, so they would not be out of sorts with him. (Nerger simply ignored that request.) He also said rather plaintively that he needed for his health a chilled bottle of champagne every morning at breakfast. (Nerger had to tell him the *Wolf* was right out of champagne.)

As the ships steamed along in tandem, or in file, the radiomen of both were listening to the traffic between Sydney and Rabaul. Where, asked Rabaul on the evening of 7 August, was *Matunga*? Radio Rabaul had been calling her all day and there was no answer. Sydney replied that Rabaul must certainly be raising the ship any moment now, for she was already late. Rabaul replied that she knew that, and that was the problem. Sydney refused to get upset at first, then did get very upset, and began showering the airwaves with calls. Searches were begun, concentrated on the area where *Matunga* had sent her last message, a few hours from the point where she had been halted by *Wolf*. But the *Wolf* and her captive were now many miles north of this area. The searches proved negative. Rabaul kept calling, to no avail. No sign of *Matunga* was found, no indication of an enemy ship or submarine in these waters.

Governments must have logical explanations for everything, illogical as these may be, and soon Australia's government was searching elsewhere than in the winds of war for the reasons for *Matunga*'s disappearance. There had been reports of an earthquake in this area of the South Pacific at about the time *Matunga* failed to respond, and now the seismologists were called upon to give their opinions: could *Matunga* have been swallowed up in the disaster? Naturally she could, said the seismologists. Naturally she was, said the government. So the cruisers were recalled, the search was ended, and the whisky, beer, wine, coal, and passengers of *Matunga* were declared to be victims of a horrible natural disaster.

Meanwhile, *Wolf* made off with her captive, evading the searchers, and a week after the capture, on 13 August, Nerger ordered the ships to heave to off a small jungled island, Waigioe, off the northwest end of New Guinea, almost on the equator. As soon as *Wolf* stopped, the derrick was put into motion, Fabeck and Stein put on their goggles and stepped into the cockpit, and were

101

hoisted over the side, to begin a scouting mission. Nerger intended to remain in this anchorage and unload *Matunga*, and he wanted to make sure he was not going to be disturbed by any prying eyes.

Captain Nerger was an old hand in the Far East, as noted, and he had learned a great deal about these waters in years past when he served in the China Squadron. When the seaplane returned with its cheery message that they were absolutely alone, the crew and prisoners thought Nerger intended to drop anchor in this relatively sheltered water on the far side of the weather gauge. Not so, the captain took the bridge, and ordered *Wolf* ahead, slow. The quartermaster steered straight for the beach, *Matunga* following puppetlike in her wake, and the fearful wondered suddenly if their captain had not gone mad, thus to beach a good ship. But as the green jungle parted to become individual trees and vines, a narrow channel opened among them, and *Wolf* began edging into a natural canal that curved around the back of a tall hill, then opened into a large, perfectly protected harbour, whose clear blue water sparkled in the equatorial sun. The jungles steamed on both sides, birds and monkeys rustled through the trees, and parrots and bright blue birds flew up, as the macaques disturbed them. On the shore, a few natives watched, wide-eyed, as the big ships invaded their home, then disappeared into the jungle, not to reappear for many hours.

The ships anchored, and as the chains sang out, Nerger issued the order to get to work unloading the *Matunga*. Leutnant Rose came off *Matunga* with copies of the cargo lists, and these were handed with the efficient snap that marked the raider to three sections of men, working under officers. Their task was to clear the *Matunga*. The stewards, firemen, and sailors of the Australian ship were brought aboard *Wolf* and sent to join the other prisoners. The German sailors stripped down to shorts and shoes, for the heat had grown almost intolerable the moment the ships stopped moving. At midday, not a leaf stirred on the island and the surface of the lagoon was absolutely glassy except where some fish rose, or along the shore where the beady eyes of a crocodile bumped up for a moment as he surveyed the ships with lofty calculation.

Mrs. Cameron, the wife of the American captain of *Beluga*, came out of her cabin, almost for the first time since entering, to greet Mrs. Flood, wife of the Australian physician, and Miss MacKenzie, who turned out to be not a maid, as Leutnant Rose had believed, but the stewardess of the *Matunga* and a person in her own right. They were greeted punctiliously as usual by Captain Nerger in his immaculate whites, who assured them they had nothing to fear from the Germans, apologized for the inconvenience offered ladies, and promised that they and the husbands of two of them would be freed just as soon as humanly possible. Meanwhile they would have to be his reluctant guests, and would have to comport themselves within the rules of a German warship. Nerger now sent a landing party ashore in a launch. The men took rifles, pistols and machetes with them, and when they landed they hacked a trail up to the top of the southern headland and established a lookout station. All but two came back, and these remained as lookouts, to be relieved every day. Nerger was taking no chances on surprise, day or night.

The prisoners had been allowed for the past few nights to come up and sleep on the poop deck, because of the intense heat below in these equatorial climes. But no more. Captain Nerger remembered very well the occurrence at Sunday Island, and he was determined that none of the prisoners should escape. This place, unlike Sunday Island, was inhabited and he could well imagine one of the Englishmen hiring a native guide to take him to civilization, and then bringing the wrath of the British navy down upon *Wolf*. So as the ship anchored, extra guards were stationed on the poop, a rope was run around the deck four feet back from the rails and stanchions were brought up to hold it, and the prisoners were ordered to stay behind the rope on pain of death, and under no conditions to talk to the natives.

The natives began swarming around the ship, within the first hour. They did not come aboard, for Captain Nerger did not want them aboard until he was ready, but they called up from their canoes, and seemed eager to trade with the crew. The trading began only at the end of the day, as the sun set below the edge of the island. That first night in Offak Bay was a horror for the prisoners. Now there were two hundred of them, and they were herded below into the prisoner's compartment in the suffocating heat, and locked in.

On coming aboard, Captain Donaldson's first remark had been about his "medicine", his second had been to ask where was his cabin. Now he discovered where it was. This prison hold was twelve feet high, forty feet long and thirty feet wide. A sheep gets sixteen square feet in a barn, or the shepherd will suffer losses; these prisoners had six square feet per man. Their compartment had been the afterhold of the freighter, and the sides tapered, as the hull curved into the stern. The steel plates were sizzling hot from the sun and with no one below it was steamy and fetid in the hold. Crammed with two hundred men, within an hour it was a foul-smelling hellhole. At first, the officers and men were segregated in the old pattern established after the incident of the armchair, but soon it became apparent this was impossible for all. The men were literally collapsing in the heat, the enlisted men were best off because the few vents into the hold were in their section, the senior officer's quarters were hottest of all.

Captain Meadows finally took action, two or three hours after the sun had gone down. He pushed his way through the crowd and accosted the German sailor who was guarding the foot of the companionway. The sailor levelled his gun at the captain, but the captain refused to give way. The sailor himself was nearly overcome but he dare not leave his post. Finally he shouted up to the deck, and was answered, and within a few moments Leutnant Oswald appeared, with one of the ship's doctors behind him.

"You have got to let us out of here," said Captain Meadows.

"Impossible," said Oswald. "Captain's order. No prisoners on deck." He smiled thinly. "You will remember what happened at Sunday Island?"

Meadows brushed him aside and spoke to the doctor.

"They'll die," he said. "They'll die like flies."

The doctor looked around nervously. He could not but agree. He implored Leutnant Oswald with his eyes.

"We shall have to go to the captain," said Oswald.

They marched off, and in half an hour returned. Captain Nerger refused to allow the prisoners on deck. However, they would make a concession, and open the main hatch cover at one corner to let some air in. That was the best the men held prisoner aboard *Wolf* could do that night. They sweated and cursed and stank, but they survived.

Next day, the prisoners began scrabbling for position. Those who held military ranks, approached Captain Nerger first, and asked special treatment on the grounds of military courtesy. Nerger sat in his cabin, his whites immaculate even in the heat, and listened. The ship's cat Eva sat nearby and washed a paw. Nerger heard, and he judged. Governor Strangman (as he called the Australian doctor) and three other Australian officers would be given quarters. So would all other naval or military officers. Three businessmen from *Matunga* also managed to get into better quarters, by claiming their only interest in going to Rabaul was to straighten out affairs for their German friends, and that they were really acting on the Kaiser's behalf.

"I should have given them all Iron Crosses," said Nerger, his eyes twinkling. "His Majesty never had such servants."

The prisoner question settled, it seemed, as best he could manage it under the circumstances, Captain Nerger devoted his full attention to pulling the ship together and moving those supplies. With the mining of New Zealand and Australian waters he had completed two phases of his campaign against the British. Now he was ready for an equally daring exploit, but it would not be right to go until *Wolf*, too, was ready. He was going to go in, alone into the heart of his enemy's stronghold, and lay a massive minefield in Singapore. It would be a feat unequalled since von Müller in *Emden* had steamed brazenly on Penang, charged into the harbour, sunk the Russian cruiser *Yemtschuk*, and the French destroyer *Mousquet*, and charged out again to safety—for a while. Captain Nerger was determined to equal von Müller's exploit, with one significant alteration: he intended to go into phase three and then go home safely to Germany to fight again.

9

On the Attack

Wolf had been at sea for nine months, and her storerooms and coal holds were very nearly empty before *Matunga* came along. From the moment of anchoring in Offak Bay the crew laboured during the daylight hours. Coal loading was begun very early in the morning, before heat made it real torture to struggle down into the bunkers of *Matunga*, load a sack of coal, carry it pickaback up the companionway across the deck, over the gangway, down into the bowels of *Wolf*, empty the sack, and then start back to do it all over again. The prisoners had one moment of happiness when they discovered that their erstwhile companions, the "neutrals" who had opted for life with the

Germans, were all in the coaling gang. It was real punishment.

While the lowest rating and the black gang coaled, others were working over other parts of *Wolf* very carefully. Drydock would have been nice, but in its absence, Nerger sent divers over the side—in full diving dress (he had forgotten nothing back at Kiel) and they went to work scraping off the accumulation of barnacles and weeds that had grown to the hull, and cut her speed by almost a third. The black gang got to work on the boilers again and the engines were overhauled, pipes replaced and great gobs of grease applied. All this was accomplished in the almost intolerable heat of the tropics, but there was one relief. Every afternoon at around four o'clock the blue sky above the bay would cloud up, then darken, and it would rain. For fifteen minutes or so the rain would pour down in sheets. So every day the work would stop at four o'clock, the men would strip, and go on deck and wash the day's accumulation of coal dust and sweat off themselves, and for a few minutes feel almost cool again.

The special attention given some members of the prison group brought others to make claims on Captain Nerger, so many that he soon became annoyed by the whole procedure. Miss MacKenzie, the stewardess, decided that since she was a prisoner of war, she no longer had any responsibility to serve the lady passengers, whose servant she had been on the ship. So she came to Nerger demanding "equal rights." Nerger's temper was frayed by the events of the past few days, and he opened up on her. She had her choice, he told Miss MacKenzie. Either she was a stewardess or a

110

free soul. If she was a stewardess, she could remain with the ladies above deck, and see to their needs. If she was a free soul she could go below with the other prisoners, all two hundred of them, all male. Miss MacKenzie decided she was still a stewardess.

So the supplies were transferred: three and a half tons of frozen meat, clothing, toilet articles, and above all lovely, lovely coal. There were eight hundred tons of coal, five hundred tons of it Westport, or cherished hot-burning hard coal. There were three horses aboard, too, and after the first day or so, the ship's doctor suggested to Nerger that they be slaughtered. They would be a great deal of trouble on the *Wolf*, they would surely die or be killed by the natives if left in the jungle of the island. They would give the prisoners and the crew fresh meat. And, said Doctor Hauswaldt, fresh meat was absolutely necessary at this time. He had not said much about it before, but there had been several mild cases of scurvy aboard, and he was much concerned about its repetition, and then an outbreak of the wasting disease. All that had saved them so far was the amount of fresh vegetables they had taken off the *Matunga* and these would soon be gone. He was particularly concerned about the prisoners, for they might die like flies, and that would be a serious matter. So the horses were killed that very day, and all hands were served horse stew that night, and horse cutlet, horse steak, roast horse for days afterwards.

On the second day in Offak Bay, tension suddenly piled up on the bridge, as the wireless officer came to report a great deal of traffic among naval vessels in the general area. Captain Nerger

111

knew that a Japanese cruiser was not far off, and a British cruiser was somewhere about, even more worrisome in a way, because he did not quite know where she was. This increase in traffic might mean that somehow, some way, the British had caught wind of his presence, and he was in no condition to move at the moment.

This tension, the extreme heat, the plaints and demands of the prisoners, caused the captain and his crew to become very nervous about prisoner behaviour. In the original landing precautions, machineguns had been placed, pointing toward the poop, on the upper works, and guards patrolled aft constantly, on the alert for any unusual movement by the prisoners. Others manned the searchlight at night, and stood by the alarm.

On the second afternoon, the prisoners were allowed above deck and they gathered on the poop, under the shelter of an awning, and smoked and talked. It was the practice of the officers to use men to guard the prisoners closely only if they spoke English, but this fact was never to be given away by actually speaking English. It had been only days before the prisoners got onto the game, and they had played it, starting rumours in front of the guards, and then waiting to see how long it took for the rumours to come back to them, usually through Leutnant von Oswald, their mentor; also to see how they magnified in passage through the ship.

This day one of the guards was leaning a little more heavily on the prisoners than usual, and one of the English sailors decided to have a little fun with him. He spun a yarn about the plans for the big prison breakout that night, how they would rush to the deck, overpower the guards, swim ashore, make their way through the jungle to the mainland of New Guinea's big island, and spill the beans about Nerger and the *Wolf*. The canny guard showed no sign of understanding. But when the prisoners went below, the guards were doubled all around the poop, and the machineguns were double-manned. The evening meal was served, darkness settled over the ship, and the prisoners went into their hammocks.

About an hour later a succession of shots rang out in the prisoners' compartment.

"Gefangenenalarm!" came the shout from the guards below.

The whole ship broke out in shouting and alarms, and Captain Nerger jumped from his bed.

"What is it?" he yelled.

Back came the excited shouts:

"The prisoners have jumped overboard and are swimming away."

On deck, Captain Nerger searched the water, as the searchlights played around the ship: not a prisoner to be seen. But the searchlights flashed and flares began to rise high above the ship, illuminating the whole area. The machineguns clattered, as the gunners fired at shadows, and then at forms that moved in the water.

Finally, about twenty minutes later, the captain put an end to it. The prisoners were roused out and counted, and none of them was missing. A few of the crocodiles who slid in and out of the mangroves on shore seemed a bit worse for wear, and the hawsers that held *Mantunga* to *Wolf* were bullet scarred and shot away in some places. The natives, who had been supplying the ship with

113

pineapples and bananas, were the real casualties of the "uprising." They disappeared that night, taking their pigs and children and everything but the palm huts along the shore, and they never returned as long as *Wolf* was there.

During the thirteen days that *Wolf* and *Matunga* lay in the lagoon together, the crew of the raider had fashioned new cabins amidships for the privileged prisoners, so the officers might have their quarters back. The women and their husbands were by far the best treated, although the Camerons and Floods had to share a makeshift cabin. But they ate in the officers' mess, after the officers had finished, and were joined there by Governor Strangman and his officers, and the privileged civilians; fourteen of them in all. The rest, some two hundred, including all the merchant ship captains except Cameron, were crowded aft.

On 25 August the unloading at *Matunga* was finished. Nerger was eager to get to sea, and into action. He gave the prisoners an indication of the power of *Wolf* when he called for gunnery practice, and for the first time the torpedo tubes were manned, and the guns all run out in unison, as *Wolf* manoeuvred in the big bay. The prisoners were impressed with the strength of the innocent looking cargo ship, and her potential for 'destruction.

Nerger was eager to get to sea for several reasons. First was his planned attack with mines on Singapore. Second was a certain nervousness lest he be discovered by the British or even the Dutch. The British had in these waters the old German patrol boat *Komet*. She was the one for whom the coal on *Matunga* was shipped. And if *Wolf* could have outmatched *Komet* in a fight still the word of it would have aroused the defences of all Asia and probably made the Singapore operation impossible. As for the Dutch, their neutrality was not regarded by Nerger as very neutral, and he suspected that if he was spotted, the result was going to be the same as a fight.

On 26 August, Captain Nerger got into the pinnace and was taken around the ship for an inspection. She had been freshly painted black, and looked very trim. Not one of the weapons showed, and to his practiced eye there was nothing amiss that would betray *Wolf*'s military bearing. Satisfied, he returned to the bridge, and gave the order to move out to sea. *Wolf* was now fairly heavily laden; *Matunga* carried only enough coal for an hour's steaming, for this was the end of her life.

Wolf moved slowly through the narrow channel to the sea, and out beyond, in the clear water, the men and the prisoners breathing a sigh of relief as for the first time in two weeks they felt the freshness of a sea breeze in their faces. *Matunga* toiled sadly behind, until they were ten miles off the coast. Then the German prize crew got into their boat and came back to the mother ship, having left two charges along the waterline, aft. A few minutes later came the explosions, muffled bangs, followed by the sounds of breaking up inside, and the Australian ship slowly went down by the stern, until the sharp bow gave a little shudder, and too, it disappeared. For a few minutes there was a swirling and a little flotsam, but very little, because the Germans had battened down all floatables inside to prevent recognizable pieces of *Matunga* from being found, and tipping off the en-

115

emy that she had disappeared so far north of her last position. Satisfied, Captain Nerger now turned his eyes west, and gave the orders to steam for Singapore. His ship was as fit as he could make her, she was as well-supplied as he could expect, and he was back on the attack.

On board the raider, the prisoners could hardly believe Nerger would be so foolhardy as to attack Singapore. The British captains knew it could not be done, for Singapore was invulnerable—the Admiralty said so. This was the most important naval base in Asia, virtually all the ships that moved from the Indian Ocean came through the Straits of Malacca, the British patrolled constantly, and there were always half a dozen big warships in Singapore harbour or at the naval base. Particularly since the United States entered the war in the spring of 1917, British power in the Pacific could be concentrated on Singapore, for the Americans covered the Philippies and China. Nor could anyone say that the British would be sleeping in Singapore harbour these days, for the mining of Colombo and Bombay had proved it could be done, and the high command was on the alert.

Yet Captain Nerger knew a good deal about the disposition of ships and the comings and goings in Singapore, because he had the mailbags from *Wairuna* and *Matunga*. Australia and New Zealand were so far from the war in Europe that no one really considered censoring homebound mail, and so Nerger had a good bit of intelligence in these bags. He knew something about the patrols, something about the habits of shipping, and the way the port was run. It was invaluable information, and without it he might well have decided

116

the risk was too great; with this information he was ready for this grand coup against the enemy.

The *Wolf* steamed now into the Banda Sea, and steamed through the Moluccas, changing course whenever a smoke plume was sighted. Captain Nerger was not looking for prizes, but trying to reach his destination without trouble. Every few hours the alarms rang and the men rushed to battle stations, as those smoke columns appeared. The routine was always the same.

"Ship in sight," came the cry, and the alarm bells began to ring. The privileged passenger-prisoners headed immediately for their cabins, as ordered. Men ran along the deck, finding their action stations, and stood there, watchful. One day, they thought they saw the *Juno*, a British cruiser with two funnels and two masts, and the gunners were ready for action. Their guns trained at 310° and they followed the other ship as she moved along the horizon. There was absolute silence at the guns and in the fire control centre, where Leutnant Witschetzky was giving a quiet succession of orders. The ship was now only two thousand yards away and still coming. Still *Wolf* kept her course (to do anything else would arouse suspicion) and with her sides up, and the guns concealed, she still looked the merchantman.

"Seventeen hundred yards," sang out the talker.

"Fifteen hundred."

Witschetzky was very excited, and he called the captain, and asked if he could open fire. Nerger was brusque, masking his own excitment and worry. No, he said, they must not fire a gun; they would not fight unless the cruiser tried to stop them. But at fifteen hundred yards, the suspense

117

growing intolerable, the English ship suddenly turned away, satisfied apparently, put on a burst of speed, and disappeared very shortly across the horizon.

The ship steamed past the green island of Amboina and then past Banda and into the Flores Sea. Four days later she passed the island of Celebes and steamed west into the Java Sea where the shipping traffic was almost continuous. Here was a harvest for a raider, tankers, small freighters, big freighters, all unsuspecting in these quiet waters for they were sure no enemy would dare venture here in the summer of 1917. Nerger gave them no thought at all. His will power was such that he was totally given over to his primary mission, the mining of Singapore with the 110 mines still aboard the *Wolf*. The raider joined the traffic, as innocent as could be, and the captain made sure that his men played the part of merchant seamen. At the signal mast, the signal officer had stowed a collection of British, American, Dutch, Swedish, and Norwegian flags, and when they came upon a vessel and it dipped its ensign Nerger would order the most appropriate of these run up. But when the other ship asked "What ship? What ship?" *Wolf* never, never answered, for that game was much too risky and would require a constant search of Lloyd's register for names of ships that might pass for *Wolf* at a distance. Even so, who was to know if the ships had been sunk in European waters or met some other disaster? To get too close and too involved was dangerous, so Captain Nerger simply let the passers-by think he had bad eye-sight or an uncommon lack of courtesy. He was far safer that way.

Through the Java Sea at ten knots, and then came the course change that took her around Borneo, the men staying low, the aeroplane knocked down and stowed, the ladies actually encouraged to promenade on deck and show themselves, to prove *Wolf*'s character as a ship of peace. On the night of 2 September, *Wolf* entered Karimata strait. This meant he was taking the southern approach, which was actually more dangerous for him than the northern, because in the south most of the traffic was Dutch and the patrol craft knew the ships and their markings. Aboard the *Wolf* Captain Meadows was taking bets that they would never get through the patrols.

"I've been at Singapore four times before the war," he said. "If you think you'll ever arrive you're crazy. In the south, in Karimata and Malacca, I know there are British and Japanese cruisers. You'll never make it. And if you do make it, by some miracle, then you'll be mousetrapped right there."

The nights were cool and clear, much clearer than Captain Nerger liked. The first night went by without incident but on the second night, *Wolf* encountered another British cruiser, which came so close alongside that he could see the light on the blacked-out ship's bridge as someone opened the chartroom door. The tension was tremendous, every man at his battle station, standing, waiting— but the British cruiser ignored them and went on without even a hail.

On the morning of 4 September, Nerger made ready for his work. One prisoner who had been sick was in sick bay; he was sent back under guard to the after compartment to join the others.

The ship was about to go into action, and there was no time to fool with prisoners, when the two doctors might have to take care of wounded German sailors. In the mine compartment the mine officer and his men adjusted the cables of the mines for the proper depth off Singapore harbour, and began moving them out on deck. The tracks were laid carefully, the mines on their little wheeled carts were brought out on deck, and all was ready. As night fell, the ship moved in south of the Anamba Islands in the South China Sea, where pass most ships from the Philippines, China and Japan, on their way to Singapore. The minelaying began here, as *Wolf* moved along, zig-zagging, dropping mines in clusters of five, then moving on. She laid several fields, and then doubled back, heading again for the strait of Malacca.

By daylight it was all over, and the innocent black cargo ship was back in the stream of traffic east of the Malacca Strait, the sweet land smells blowing in the nostrils of the lookouts as they stood at their posts. Below, the prisoners were taking bets on whether or not Captain Nerger would now head for a Dutch port and voluntary internment. It was, of course, impossible for him ever to get back to Germany, and why should he commit suicide? On the bridge, there was no thought of taking internment. Captain Nerger was examining his situation carefully, and making his plans. His primary task had now been accomplished precisely as his orders had demanded. His secondary task was to go a-raiding. He had enough coal to run for six weeks at cruising speed. He would pick up more as he went along. The rumours at the scuttlebutt were so strong about internment that he felt inclined to dispel them, so he made one of his infrequent announcements to the effect that *Wolf* was going home, not into some foreign neutral port, and for his trouble he received the cheers and grins of the crew. They now would sail anywhere with Captain Nerger, fully confident that he would take them safely back to the Fatherland.

Down below, in the prisoners' compartment, Captain Meadows began hedging his bets.

10

The Raider's Teeth

Captain Nerger had chosen his approach and escape route with the care of genius. He was well away, in Dutch waters, when the first mine exploded, and the British merchant ship *Port Kembla* put out the dread cry: "I have struck a mine and am sinking."

Tugs, fireboats, and rescue ships came to her assistance, but before any arrived, *Port Kembla* went down. Then came another distress signal from the British ship *Brodholm*, which had struck another of Captain Nerger's mines, and was seriously damaged, although tugs arrived and managed to beach her on the Isle of Anamba. Then, even more alarming news: the Japanese battleship

Haruna struck one of the mines. She was too big and too strong to sink, but she was damaged, and the embarrassment to the British naval authorities was intense. What could not happen had happened. An enemy ship had somehow penetrated the impenetrable defences of Singapore and dropped mines almost in the harbour's mouth.

During the five days after the minelaying, *Wolf* reversed her course, into East Indian waters, and as the ship moved along the edge of Borneo, there came an incident that was to prove very important. Captain Meadows had never stopped his practice of dropping messages over the side of the *Wolf* whenever he felt there was a chance one bottle might reach land. One day off Borneo he prepared a note describing the mining and *Wolf*'s activities since he had been aboard (he was the first captured) and concealed the bottle in an armload of laundry he pretended to take up on deck for washing.

When the time came for the prisoners to be allowed up on deck, Captain Meadows took his bundle and started up the companionway. At the top he was spotted by Quartermaster Brandes, one of the guards, who noted suspiciously that here was something new and unwanted. Meadows mingled with the others, joined the "Captain's Club" to sit and play cards and gossip, and tried to avoid attracting attention. But Brandes' eye was on him nonetheless. Then came the call, about nightfall: "Return the prisoners."

Meadows began shuffling toward the rail, planning to throw his bundle overboard. Brandes moved meaningfully across the deck, toward Meadows. Meadows raised his bundle: Brandes raised his hands. "Stop!" he shouted, and grabbed the English captain. But Meadows was a big strong man, and he wrenched his arms free and dumped the parcel overboard.

Furious now, Brandes hustled Captain Meadows to the bridge, to report this disgraceful affair to Captain Nerger. The German captain began questioning him: was he sending messages overboard? Who were his contacts? Meadows solidly refused to admit anything. He was taken to a small guarded room below decks, put under double guard, and left to think. But he would not talk and finally Nerger tired of it and told the executive officer to send him back with the other prisoners. Nothing had come of the messages anyhow, he decided.

That last was not quite true. The English captain was confined to his quarters—he no longer had the privilege of going on deck to watch the sunset and the seagulls or to breathe the fresh air of the sea. But somehow he managed to get one more bottle overboard a few days later, and that bottle was found, and the message transmitted to the Admiralty. Fortunately for Captain Nerger it really made no difference; the bottle was picked up by a native of Toli Toli, an island in the Celebes, in December 1917, and took a month to get to England because the British consul in Batavia did not believe it. By this time Nerger was far, far away from these waters.

Other wheels were grinding to bring about the end of *Wolf* in these summer days, and they were far more dangerous to the German raider. Although the story of the loss of *Matunga* through underwater earthquake was peddled to the public that summer, the naval authorities themselves really never believed it, and some bright people in naval intelligence were putting two and two together. Here was the *Matunga* gone. And then there was the disturbing news that *Wairuna* had not shown up at the Panama Canal, where she was supposed to be weeks before; indeed, no one in the world had caught sight of her since she sailed from New Zealand, outward bound. On 31 August, the Australian naval command set up a special lookout system in the Torres Straits. The cruiser *Encounter* was dispatched to the Russel Islands, to make a thorough search with the Japanese cruisers *Hirado* and *Chikuma*. Three days later, Admiral Grant of the China Station sent the *Psyche* and *Fantome* to Thursday Island, and the *Suffolk* to the Andaman and Nicobar Islands, to search for a German surface raider.

Psyche and *Fantome* steamed first for Timor by way of the Java Sea, and it is almost a wonder that they did not run squarely into *Wolf*, for she was just ahead of them. They used the Sunda Strait, but Nerger had a hunch that this was just the wrong thing for him to do at this time, and he refrained from taking the ordinary, safe route. He kept to the east of Java, picking a route in consultation with his navigator, that led through dangerous waters, past reefs and rocks at night, where navigation and luck were his only friends.

Radio traffic out of Singapore, much of it now in naval code, indicated to him that the fat was certainly in the fire after the mining of the approaches to Singapore. That port's authorities were crying now for minesweepers, but an embarrassed Admiralty had to tell them they would

126

have to wait; no one had envisaged a need for minesweepers in Asiatic waters in 1917, and the nearest were at Malta and could not be dispatched for several weeks. So the area around Anamba Island became poisoned water, and many a ship was delayed weeks or months, or never arrived at all, because of Captain Nerger and the *Wolf*.

At Whitehall, the admirals were now certain they had a raider with which to deal, but they were playing with information the way a child plays with a jigsaw puzzle. Here were the puzzling facts, as presented to the board.

1 A raider was reported in the western approaches to the Panama Canal in May.
2 A burning ship had been sighted east of Christmas Island on 19 June.
3 The *Wairuna* had disappeared en route from Auckland to San Francisco.
4 A burning ship had been seen south of New Caledonia.
5 A burning derelict had been sighted east of New Caledonia.
6 A burning vessel had been sighted off Jarvis Island in the Central Pacific.
7 A suspicious steamer had been reported off Port Macquarie.
8 A black steamer had been reported off Laughlan Island.
9 A suspicious steamer had been reported off the Russel Islands.
10 The *Cumberland* had gone down, and there were some in the navy who did not believe the story of "internal explosion."
11 *Matunga* had vanished without a trace on her way to Rabaul.

12 Not a single survivor had been discovered any-
    where from any of these missing vessels.

The Admiralty concluded that a plot of the activity indicated there was a raider abroad, that she
had moved across the Pacific from east to west in
May and June and July, and had been operating
in the Coral Sea between New Guinea and Australia since that time.

So the search was on, but for many wrong reasons. *Wolf* had no connection with the Panama
Canal. That was Count von Luckner in the *Seeadler*, a sturdy sailing ship, who had run the
blockade in the second week of December 1916,
just as *Wolf* was going out. He had then sailed
around Cape Horn in frightful weather, through a
British blockade, and had then taken several
prizes in South American waters. The hulk burning east of Christmas Island was obviously also
one of *Seeadler's* victims, although this was not
obvious at all to the British naval authorities, who
knew nothing of the reality of either of these
raiders. If the truth had been known, the fact was
that of the twelve points studied by the Admiralty, only three indicated *Wolf*: the mysterious
disappearance of *Wairuna* and of *Matunga*, and
the strange sinking of *Cumberland*.

But even in error, the British were aroused, and
began to take action to stop the ravages of the
"raider." As they acted, Count von Luckner was
shipwrecked, his vessel driven ashore on the
French island of Mopeha north of the Cook Island
group by a tidal wave, and he set sail in an open
boat to try to capture another ship and continue
raiding. They sailed two thousand three hundred
miles, decided to land on the island of Katafanga

near the Fijis, and instead landed on Wakaya on 21 September. By this time, *Wolf* was far away.

Having dodged the cruisers searching for him in the Java Sea, Nerger moved off Sumatra, and near Soerabaya on Sunday 9 September, he encountered a number of ships, which he met with his usual deceptive, half-blind friendliness, running up a succession of neutral or allied flags, and ignoring all hails. They steamed close to Lombok Island, close enough to see the mountains clearly, and the houses of the planters and huts of the natives, and clear of Lombok Strait, they were in the open sea. The passage was made at night, the ship totally blacked out, the prisoners shut in their hold without the grace of that open hatch. Then came the pitching and the heavy breeze that told every seaman aboard that *Wolf*, having picked her way among the island chains all these days, was now out again in the open sea. Next morning tension was remarkably relaxed aboard the ship. The prisoners were almost welcomed on deck, their jailers were laughing and chatting among themselves; even Captain Nerger wore a smile. For now he had many days of open steaming ahead of him before he had to worry about the enemy in strength. *Wolf* loafed along at half speed to conserve coal, and even the weather was good for them, bright and sunny and not too warm.

Yet within a week, Nerger was worrying again. It was coal, as usual, that brought the deep furrows to his brow. *Wolf* used up some thirty tons of coal a day at half speed, thirty-five tons at eight knots, which was her normal cruising speed, and sixty tons a day if she had to steam at full speed. Calculating, the captain estimated that he had now used up all the coal he had acquired from *Matunga*. She had, in effect, given him the power to move in and mine the enemy of Singapore, but he was going to have to find another donor to give him the life-blood to get *Wolf* back home to Germany. Almost immediately the doctors reported other alarming news. The fresh food of *Matunga* had long since given out and the horsemeat was gone. There were six hundred people aboard this ship and that meant tons of provisions. With the absence of fresh foods, the prisoners were beginning to show signs of scurvy. If the prisoners were in such sore straits, eating the same ration as the sailors, then it would not be long before Nerger would have a truly serious problem on his hands.

Then one of the prisoners died. The cause of the death was officially listed as a heart attack—the man had a history of heart disease—but Nerger could not be sure it was not a death attributable in part at least to the old blight of the sailing ships. He buried the prisoner with full military honours. Since he was an American, the Stars and Stripes was draped over the shroud before it dropped into the sea. Nerger was there in dress uniform, with all his officers, and they paid their respects. He gave no sign of the worries that were building up in him.

In the third week of September, the radio traffic buzzed day and night in the Pacific regions with a tremendous stir. A raider had been captured! Actually the capture had been that of Count von Luckner and the crew he had taken in his open boat. They had gone aboard a two-masted schooner at Wakaya, with the intention of seizing the vessel when it got into the open sea. They had told a cock and bull story about being Norwegian sailors who had taken a ship's lifeboat on an excursion and then missed their ship. The captain of the sailing ship had listened and smiled and nodded—and gone straight to the authorities. So von Luckner and his men were captured, and the British were aroused.

On 24 September, the *Brisbane* was sent to the Solomons to try to find von Luckner's raider. The *Encounter* and the *Hirado* went to Fiji, where von Luckner was being held, and began questioning him. Von Luckner. Aha! The Australian press picked up the story, and so did the newspapers of New Zealand and soon both colonies were thoroughly aroused against the "damned Huns" who had murdered the poor innocents of *Wairuna*. That was the charge in the newspapers, and when the British moved von Luckner and his men from Suva to Auckland, New Zealand tempers were thoroughly aroused.

Von Luckner said repeatedly that he had never heard of the *Wairuna*, and that his sailing ship had certainly not sunk her. The British and the New Zealanders believed none of his story. Angry crowds began to gather around the prison camp on the island of Somes. Von Luckner and his first leutnant were moved to a smaller island at the entrance to Auckland harbour. But the rage of the people continued; they packed the government buildings in Auckland, and paraded in the streets demanding that von Luckner and his crew of pirates be hanged.

The authorities were very nearly panic-stricken. Von Luckner was moved to the naval barracks at Devonport Torpedo Yard, under a total ban of secrecy. But someone leaked the story and crowds surrounded the yard. The authorities moved him again, to the island of Motuihi; again the word got out. They were taken back to Auckland and kept in a guarded railroad freight car on a siding, with two beds for furniture. They were moved to Wellington and secreted in the old Danish barracks. Finally, von Luckner was taken aboard a cruiser in the harbour and questioned by Sir Hall Thompson, captain of His Majesty's Navy and commander of the forces of New Zealand, to testify at the inquiry into the disappearance of the *Wairuna*. Von Luckner gave his word of honour as a German officer and nobleman that he had never heard of the *Wairuna*, and Captain Thompson accepted it, but not totally. Then, to check out the von Luckner story, the Japanese cruiser *Usuma* was sent to Mopeha. Meanwhile the officer von Luckner had left in charge of the crew of *Seeadler* when he went to forage for another ship, had decided to take a boat and head for Easter Island, and had gone, leaving their prisoners on Mopeha behind them. The prisoners confirmed von Luckner's story, the authorities finally believed him, and now they came to the final conclusion that there was another raider at large in southern waters.

As all this was happening, and the radio carried the reports of von Luckner's capture, Captain Saunders, much lamented by the crowds of angry New Zealanders, was not lying in a bed of seaweed, his eyes picked out by coral fish. Even if his lot was not a very happy one, he was alive and relatively well in the after hold of the *Wolf*, and the same was true of his officers and crew. They were still hoping that Captain Meadows' bet on the internment of *Wolf* was correct, but the navigators among them, figuring they were now about off the tip of Ceylon again, were not at all comforted by the direction in which Captain Nerger was moving. He should be moving back to the Dutch East Indies, where the neutrals were. The prisoners were even more downcast on 26 September, when the order came to bring the little seaplane up out of the hold and put it together on deck. Raiding again, that was the ticket, and now it was stamped.

On 27 September *Wolf* was sailing through the Maldive Islands on a southwesterly course, when suddenly came the cry from the forward lookouts:

"Rauchwolke in sicht!"

Immediately Captain Nerger was on the bridge, ordering the seaplane into the air, to take a good look, and the pilots were soon aloft, circling to gain altitude. They returned in half an hour to report with some satisfaction that they had spotted a freighter steaming along twelve miles away, following the same southwest course. This was easy, it was simply a question of following and overtaking, and without a change of course there was a very good chance that the other ship would never suspect anything at all until those false sides fell down with a clash that sent shivers through the hearts of the prisoners just below the after guns, and the warning shot was fired across the bow. The ship was first sighted around noon. By midafternoon the hull itself was visible. For psychological value as much as anything else, Nerger launched the seaplane again, and then moved in for the capture. He came up to within 2,500 yards of the other ship, without attracting attention.

"Stop immediately. Do not use your radio."

Now Captain Nerger could see that the ship bore the name *Hitachi Maru*, which meant she was Japanese and one of the enemy. Also she carried a gun on the poop.

Nerger ran up the Imperial German battle ensign, and fired a warning shot across the bow of the other ship. Suddenly the other went into reverse, backing around so that her gun would train on *Wolf*.

There was no time to be lost. Nerger acted. The crew had been keeping their heads down as they had learned long before, but every gun was manned and ready.

"Fire a salvo!" shouted Nerger.

Leutnant Witschetzky gave the command.

"Eight hundred yards, salvo, fire!"

Four of the seven big guns roared out. *Wolf* carried the guns, but she had never fired them together before, and the result was startling aboard the raider. She reeled back to port, rivets came loose, bolts fell clanking to the deck, and wooden splinters filled the air as the ship shrieked her protest. The hold where the prisoners were kept filled with dust and they began coughing and choking.

"Another!" came the order.

Witschetzky had seen his first salvo hit home, smashing into the hull and deck of the other ship. He watched through his binoculars as the enemy gun-aimer turned the poop gun toward *Wolf*, then a shell struck nearby, and he collapsed, as did the three others in the crew. The gun was hidden in a cloud of smoke for a moment, but four other sailors rushed up to it as soon as the smoke cleared away, and began turning the weapon toward *Wolf*.

"Fire!"

The second salvo roared out. On *Wolf* the flimsy wooden partitions built for the prisoners collapsed and made rubble on the decks. On *Hitachi Maru* the second gun crew fell, and did not get up again, and a fire began somewhere amidships.

"Stop shooting at the hull," ordered Captain Nerger. "We need this ship. Don't sink her."

From the *Wolf*'s radio room, out burst a radioman heading for the bridge.

"She's using her radio," he cried as he came running. "She's sending for help."

Nerger's face grew grim. He could not stand for this; if she continued to broadcast, *Wolf*'s position would be known, and all the British might of the Indian Ocean would be turned against him. Then his chances of ever seeing Germany again were almost nil.

"Put a salvo into the bridge," he said.

The third salvo rang out, and one shell passed through the funnel, tearing half of it away. Men were now launching lifeboats from the Japanese ship, and forms could be seen jumping overboard. But a third guncrew had moved to man the gun, even as the wounded men wriggled on the deck to get clear of this position of danger. The radio had stopped now, but the steamer gave a lurch forward, as someone ordered full speed ahead. Nerger was grim. This slaughter was not to his liking.

"Another salvo," he commanded, "on the bridge again."

This fourth salvo landed on the boat deck, and burst near a group of men who were just getting into a lifeboat. The carnage was fearful; from *Wolf* the men could see halves of bodies fly into the air, and blood stained the broken lifeboat crimson. Just at this moment, the seaplane came in low over the *Hitachi Maru* and dropped two bombs. That was the final blow; the engines were stopped, and someone went to the mast and pulled down the Japanese flag. The ship was giving up.

"Hold your fire," ordered Captain Nerger. The guncrews aboard *Wolf* stood eagerly, waiting a new order, their guns warm from the firing for this first time on this voyage.

The Japanese ship slowed to a stop. A broken steam line sent forth a cloud of white that hissed through the vitals and emerged from ventilators and companionways. Now a hundred men were over the side, many of them in the water, swimming and crying out for help. With the last salvo, Nerger ordered away the boarding party, and Leutnant Rose and his crew were on their way to the other ship, passing the boats, particularly one boat in which a group of passengers were bailing with sun helmets to keep afloat.

"Boat crews away," ordered Nerger, sending his ship's boats to help the struggling people in the water. But the *Wolf*'s gunners continued to man their guns, Witschetzky keeping them on the alert.

Wolf's boat crews pulled hard, as if they had been rescuing survivors all their lives, dredging dank forms from the water and piling them in the bottom of the boats. In half an hour the passengers and crew of *Hitachi Maru* began coming aboard *Wolf*, herded down into the empty mine compartment until they could be sorted out, men, women and children, English civilians, British and Indian soldiers, Portuguese soldiers, Chinese, Japanese and Indian travellers. For this was a mail steamer bound from Yokohama to London, the 6,500-ton twin screw ship owned by Nippon Yusen Kaisha. She had called at Hong Kong, and then at Singapore and finally at Colombo. One of these unfortunates had a unique story to tell when he came aboard *Wolf*. This English civil servant had left India the year before for home, had been aboard a ship torpedoed by a submarine in the English channel, had been bombed by Zeppelins while in London, very nearly being struck by a bomb (as practically no one else was) had returned to India aboard the steamer *Mongolia*, which had struck one of *Wolf*'s mines on 26 June and gone down with a loss of twenty-six lives, had spent some time in a lifeboat and contracted a severe case of nervous exhaustion because of it, and had taken passage on *Hitachi Maru* to escape the rigours of war.

Of the hundred people struggling in the water all were saved but two Japanese sailors, whose drowned bodies were brought into the sick bay to be sewn in canvas for their long rest in the deeps. Leutnant Rose, meanwhile, had gained the bridge of *Hitachi Maru*, to find it totally deserted, save for one man, the captain. On the deck, Rose saw a dozen silent forms clustered around the gun, witnesses, albeit tragic ones, to the accuracy of *Wolf*'s gunnery. The wireless room was wrecked, the operator dead over his broken machine. There were dead men on the bridge and on the decks. Rose put part of his crew to work tidying up, getting the bodies overboard as gently and quickly as he could. As for himself, he turned his attention to the captain, and asked him courteously to come to the *Wolf*.

"Please let me go down with my ship," said Captain Tominaga. "I can never return to Japan now. I would prefer to die."

Rose argued with the captain, but vainly. Captain Tominaga was determined not to leave the bridge, and it took three stout German sailors to overpower him and carry him forcibly into the boat and back to the bridge of the *Wolf*, where Captain Nerger stood fretfully, waiting. It was high time to be at sea. That wireless signal, even if interrupted, could spell trouble. They were four hundred miles west-southwest of Colombo, in the middle of the Maldives, though land was not in sight. Worse, they were in the middle of the Colombo-South Africa sea lane, and at any time a merchantman might come along, or far more deadly, a convoy which would include a British cruiser or more. Rose came aboard with bad news. The Japanese captain was part of it, but worse was the information that that first salvo had damaged the *Hitachi Maru*'s rudder, and the ship could not be steered until it was repaired. Nerger gave an angry shake of his head, and then detailed a crew from deck and engine room to move across the water and work like demons to get that ship under way. He spared no expletives in explaining how great was the need for haste.

Nerger then gave orders for burial of all the dead, not in the fashion Rose had anticipated, but in true military spirit. The bodies and parts of bodies aboard *Hitachi Maru* were sewn into hammocks, and Captain Nerger and his men assembled in military formation on the deck of the raider, while the prize crew lined up aboard the *Hitachi Maru*, and the bodies were consigned to the depths of the sea with a short prayer. For two anxious hours they lay in the dangerous sealane while the rudder of the captured ship was repaired and broken steam line patched up. Then the ships got under way, Leutnant Rose aboard the *Hitachi Maru*, now wondering why she was ever captured, for she could do fourteen knots to *Wolf's* ten. Detail under control, Captain Nerger now had time to spare for Captain Tominaga, a handsome tall Japanese, who looked much more like a middle-aged English captain than an Oriental. Tominaga's whole demeanour and behaviour had been puzzling.

"Why did you fire your gun?" asked Nerger.

"We didn't, we just tried," said the Japanese captain.

"Why did you signal that you were stopping and then try to fight?"

"We were ordered by Tokyo to fight U-boats," said Tominaga. "I had to fight."

"You are the captain of a commerical liner, and under the rules of warfare you are not allowed to carry guns," said Nerger coldly. "Couldn't you tell that it would be useless to resist? You sacrificed the lives of thirty men."

Captain Tominaga was deeply moved, and Nerger could get no more out of him. The Japanese bowed his head, his face set, and would not talk at all. Nerger had him taken below to the mine compartment with the others from *Hitachi Maru*. He must be about his Emperor's business, and had no time for philosophical argument about the rights or wrongs of behaviour. The two ships got under way just about dark, and steamed all night to be away from the sea lane. As dawn broke, Nerger sent the seaplane aloft, to scout the outlying Maldive atolls. Again his long experience in the far east was paying off; he was in water he knew. The pilots returned to report that there was no sign of shipping in the ocean ahead and nothing in the lagoon of the island he had chosen for his anchorage while he stripped *Hitachi Maru.*

Wolf steamed cautiously through the reef into the lagoon, and anchored. *Hitachi Maru* moved up next to her. At eight o'clock that night, Captain Nerger went aboard the captured ship to see for himself what he had and what use he might make of her. He could see the work of his guns, and they had done considerable damage. But the ship could be made seaworthy, and she was indeed a prize. She was faster than *Wolf.* But her cargo was what interested him. It would be like a Christmas present to Germany to have it: crude rubber from the Indies, silk, rice, beans, flour, copper bars, brass plates, fittings and a hundred other things Germany needed very badly to pursue the war. For three years the Central Powers had been virtually cut off from the trade of the world, and the shortages of rubber, copper and other war materials were hurting. Perhaps, however, the people of Germany would welcome the tea more than anything else, since at home even before Neger left, they had been reduced to drinking bark teas and camomile teas, and simply going without. Nerger grimaced as he moved about the ship. Pools of blood still lay on the decks, and the damage was emphasized by flies around clots of flesh that still had not been cleaned up in the hurry. As he toured the ship, Nerger noted one final item on the manifest: she carried thousands of cases of canned crab and lobster from Japan, bound for England.

Such delicacies, and the necessities of war, caused Captain Nerger to calculate just what chances he might have of getting *Hitachi Maru* to Germany. He could spare the crew, even a hundred men if necessary. He could get rid of all the women and children by putting them aboard this ship, and most of the prisoners as well. The prisoners were now becoming a serious problem for him, and Dr. Hauswaldt, the chief surgeon, had just been telling him that scurvy would break out any day unless something was done to alleviate the crowding and the food problem. The cargo, the Japanese purser had told Rose, was worth a million pounds sterling. Nerger knew better: in Germany it was worth fifty million marks. On his wanderings in the captive ship, Nerger made up his mind. He would move her back to Germany. Then he began to plan.

First of all, *Hitachi Maru* must be repaired, brought into shape to sail again alone. Cement was brought up from the hold of *Wolf*, and steel plate and wooden battens, and the repairs began, even as the essential foodstuffs and war supplies of the Japanese ship, save coal, were moved over to *Wolf*. Some prisoners and the people of the *Hitachi Maru* were also moved back to that ship, for *Wolf* must now go out into the sea lanes and seek enough coal to take both ships back to Germany. The

military prisoners—soldiers, sailors and men of
military age—were kept aboard *Wolf*, lest they try
an uprising against a smaller crew. But *Wolf* rid
herself of nineteen women and two baby girls. Captain and Mrs. Cameron went aboard. So did Major
Flood and his wife, for Flood would be medical
officer, an American and his wife who had come
aboard the Japanese ship at Singapore, men over
seventy (which included Captain Rugg of the *Dee*)
and boys under fifteen. The difference was not so
great, in numbers, but having the women off his
back was a tremendous relief to Nerger. The only
one he was sorry to lose was little Anita Cameron,
daughter of the captain of the *Beluga*, who had
scampered about the ship for nearly three months,
even invading Captain Nerger's privacy, as no
other aboard *Wolf* dared do, save Eva the cat.
Nerger had grown very fond of the little girl and
would miss her.

Nerger had to move fast. Here at Suvadiva (that
was the name of the atoll he had chosen) he was
in an exposed position, for he was on the southern
flank of the Maldives, a British possession, and
this atoll might be checked out by a British
cruiser at any time, although it was virtually
deserted for the moment, with only a handful of
natives living on the shores of the lagoon. Even so,
in these three days, there was time for some explo-
ration of the island, and some contact with the
people who lived there. Most of the people lived
on the island of Dewadu. They were good looking
brown people, a mixture of Arab and Malay types,
who wore sarongs and were great sailors and
fishermen. One day one of the canoes came to the

ship, and a party of highly dressed dignitaries came aboard, representative of the king of Dewadu, who offered Nerger a white chicken in salutation. The emissaries talked for a while, and then asked if Nerger could send them his doctor to treat some sick people.

Nerger dispatched a party, led by Leutnant Witschetzky, and Leutnant Stein, to accompany the young ship's surgeon, Dr. Biester, inland to see what he could do for the people. They went inland, armed with trade goods and medicines, to a village, built along a pretty street, set in a palm forest centred around a small mosque. The doctor did what he could for the eye disease that seemed to afflict so many of the people. He was more successful in setting broken legs and treating suppurating wounds. Witschetzky and the others tried to trade rupees and pocket handkerchiefs for eggs, without much success, and then they went back to the ship with the gratitude of the king of Dewadu.

On 3 October, *Wolf* got up steam, and steamed out of the lagoon, past the inlets of Nilando and Dandu into the open sea, leaving Leutnant Rose and the prize crew, much augmented by repair specialists and extra guards, to handle *Hitachi Maru* and put her in good condition before *Wolf* returned with a new prize bearing the coal both ships needed. Nerger sailed out into the middle of the Colombo-Africa track—and found nothing. He sailed north—nothing. He sailed south—nothing.

On the second night they came upon the motorship *Peru*, but she was Danish and neutral. The officer of the watch suggested to Nerger that she must be carrying contraband, bound for Britain or her allies; the Germans were ever more certain that all the neutrals served England secretly. But Nerger would not violate his rules of war. *Peru* signalled them as dusk fell, and they did not answer. *Peru* then got on the wireless, identified herself, showed all her lights, and asked *Wolf* for identification. Nerger did not answer. *Peru* asked again. "Show your lights," she demanded. Nerger turned off the track and steamed dead south, Nerger's junior officers wondering if perhaps they should have attacked her.

Within hours they had the answer: *Wolf* passed by a larger ship, much larger than she was, a ship blacked out, which indicated a belligerent and a ship on which Nerger and his officers could see the shapes of the guns. *Wolf* slowed deferentially, playing the part of the wobbling merchantman, and the big auxiliary cruiser, for that is what Nerger was certain she was, steamed swiftly on, paying no attention.

Time was working against Captain Nerger right now. *Hitachi Maru* was expected at Lourenço Marques in Delagoa Bay any day, and she was carrying mail for the Japanese cruiser *Tsushima*, which had been assigned to the Delagoa Bay base. Soon, very soon, the word would come that *Hitachi Maru* was missing, and *Tsushima* would have a very personal stake in finding her. A week went by in which Captain Nerger found no victims, and then the moment he had been dreading arrived. The radio operators had been alerted to listen on all frequencies for anyone calling *Hitachi Maru*, and on the sixth night they heard the call, repeated by several stations. The Japanese mail ship was overdue, Lourenço Marques was worried about her, and the hunt would soon be on. It was time to be away.

Nerger had moved back ever closer to Suvadiva atoll, and now he sped there as quickly as his engines would drive the half-fouled plates of *Wolf*. Next morning, he launched the seaplane with a message for Leutnant Rose—Nerger was much too cautious to use the wireless to send any message: *"Japanese cruisers are searching for you. Leave Suvadiva at once."*

He did not steam in; it was too dangerous to be caught inside the reef, for if a British cruiser came up he would not have any chance of escaping, or even of fighting effectively. In a few hours Leutnant Rose had got up steam, weighed anchor, and the *Hitachi Maru* left her temporary haven, joining *Wolf* inside. Together they steamed south, outside the shipping lanes.

No one except Captain Nerger had the slightest idea of what he planned to do, and he did not speak of his plans. So as far as officers, men, and prisoners were concerned, they were sailing into limbo. The supply situation was growing serious, in spite of what they had picked up from the passenger-cargo ship. Nerger tried the best he could to make things easier; he unbent to ration out the whisky and other liquors to crew and captives. He was very much afraid that the crew would break into the huge liquor stores he had taken from *Matunga* and rationing it out seemed the safest and quickest way of getting rid of it.

The women off the ship, life on *Wolf* was not quite so uplifting, perhaps, but it was a good deal easier for crew and captain, and it reflected itself in their attitude toward the prisoners. The first group, mostly Europeans, continued to live in their after hold. The Japanese and others from the *Hitachi Maru* occupied the mine compartment, and Captain Tomanaga refused Nerger's offer to join the other ship captains in their quarters, but elected to remain with his own men. He seemed happy enough, resigned to the loss of his ship, and joined the others in amusing themselves by making elaborate kites and games of paper and wood; indeed the Japanese adjusted themselves far better to the prisoner's life than did the Europeans. Crew and prisoners were amused by a virtual menagerie of pets collected from the various captures. There were no fewer than seven dogs aboard *Wolf*, and innumerable cats, so many animals that in the book he later wrote about his exploits, Captain Nerger devoted an entire chapter to the menagerie, telling more about the animals than about some of his exploits: he said virtually nothing about the Singapore adventure except that he mined the area.

It was typical, for Nerger was a kindly man in a cold and demanding service, the German Imperial Navy. He could show in his leniency to the menagerie a human side that German naval tradition denied him among crew or prisoners, or even his officers. The captain is always alone, the naval captain more alone than any other, and the German naval captain the most lonely of all, for almost any sign of humanity he might give could be construed as weakness, and the Germans were never so sure of themselves at sea that any weakness was allowed to show. So *Wolf* sported a private zoo that ranged from canaries to a wild boar named Jumbo and a gibbon named Fips who lived for a while in the piano in the officer's mess, then moved to the rabbit hutch and finally ended up in the engine room. If humanly possible, Nerger was going to get them all back to the Fatherland.

11

The Hunter Hunted

Hitachi Maru was supposed to arrive off the Cape of Good Hope on 15 October, and when she did not show up the Japanese became very concerned. Unlike British merchantmen, whose captains had a good deal of freedom of movement, Japanese ships were given a tight schedule; if they did not keep it, something was definitely wrong. Not long after the disappearance of the *Wolf* and her captive into the blue, the Japanese merchant ship *Chikuzen Maru* stopped in at Suvadiva, and the sailors who went ashore were astonished to find Japanese clogs and other evidences of their culture in these strange islands. They were sure, then, that a Japanese ship had called here, but when they questioned the natives all they could learn was that two ships were in the harbour for a while, that the people aboard them spoke English, and that they went away. A British cruiser that called in at the islands quite by chance learned nothing at all, because the shore party neglected to ask any questions.

By 20 October, five days after *Hitachi Maru*'s scheduled arrival date at the cape, the wind was most certainly up. The Japanese government was not used to its mail steamers missing schedules. *Tsushima* began a determined search of the area, visiting Simonstown, Bedeque, Mozambique, Mahé, Mauritius, and Durban, and searching the islets in every one of these areas. Captain Nerger, of course, had no way of knowing precisely what was happening, but his intuition told him that the search would be long and diligent, and that he must use every bit of his craft to escape capture. The allies had some twenty ships and many small ones in the area *Wolf* was passing through; they had ten cruisers patrolling off the eastern coast of Africa, and three off the Cape of Good Hope, plus the Japanese. These ships represented the gauntlet Nerger must run if he expected to reach Germany. And take along a captive ship, too? That thought was very much in Captain Nerger's mind as he moved westward. He soon discovered to his horror that while *Hitachi Maru* made a good three knots more than *Wolf*, she also used about a third more coal. Unless he could find a fat prize immediately his plans must be jettisoned.

On 20 October, as the search for *Hitachi Maru* grew frantic, Nerger ordered the two ships into the deserted atoll of one of the Cargados Carajos island group, five hundred miles east of Madagascar, and the same distance from Mauritius. He now had many problems that had to be solved. For two weeks Nerger had been steering an erratic course across the Indian Ocean, steering west, then southwest, then east, zig-zagging in and out of the steamer lanes, hoping to catch a prize that would give them all the coal they needed. But Nerger's luck did not hold here, and he was brought to a standstill with the terrible news from Dr. Hauswaldt that disease had begun to break out in the ship.

Dr. Hauswaldt had been expecting trouble ever since they picked up the *Hitachi Maru*. Gloomily, he had been predicting outbreak of scurvy weeks earlier, but *Hitachi Maru* brought with her a whole new list of diseases, dhobi itch, that irritating skin rash that passed from one person to another, gonorrhoea, syphilis, and beriberi. One Asian passenger died from berberi a few days after the capture of the Japanese ship; he had the disease in him when he came aboard, of course, but Dr. Hauswaldt did not have the materials to treat it properly, and the man swelled up like a balloon, became paralysed, and finally died of heart failure.

As Captain Nerger was moving toward Cargados Carajos group, trying to decide what to do, there came even more unwelcome news from the medicos. Dr. Hauswaldt appeared on the bridge with his face long and one dreadful word in his mouth: typhus. Aboard a ship as in a jail, there are few more frightening diseases. It is carried by fleas, and lice, and Nerger knew very well that his holds were alive with fleas and lice. Two Japanese had come down with typhus, Dr. Hauswaldt said, and unless something was done immediately the captain could expect scourge to come to the ship, and perhaps kill every man. What could he do? Could he innoculate, asked the captain. No, replied the medico, there was no prevention for typhus; he could innoculate everyone with typhoid injections, for what good that would do. Good, said Nerger, it was to be done at once. And what else? The real answer, if there was one, was to clean the ship of lice and fleas, and isolate the sick. So the two typhus cases suddenly disappeared from *Wolf*, and none of the crew or passengers, as the prisoners might be called, ever knew what had happened to them. The medics began a scouring programme; hot water was boiled all day, every man, woman and child was stripped and clothing was boiled, and strong disinfectant was poured over their heads.

Nerger pulled in to the Cargados Carajos group, to anchor, consider, clean up, and regroup. They anchored off Cocos Island, the big hawsers looped between the ships, for the anchorage was none too sure, sheltered only by a crescent shaped reef that let the heavy Indian Ocean swell pass over and made them roll dreadfully, particularly in a southeast wind. On the morning of the 21 October, Captain Nerger was in a particularly vile mood, and no one who did not need his orders went anywhere near him; he had just taken the unhappy decision to sink the *Hitachi Maru*, his fondest hopes gone spinning, simply because he could not find a coal ship.

The Japanese treasure ship was unloaded as far

as possible, and the copper and the silk and the parts of the cargo that would be most valuable to Germany's war machine were transferred to *Wolf*, stowed down in the lowest holds. There was more bad news. The refrigerating machinery of *Hitachi Maru* had been damaged by gunfire in the battle with *Wolf*. It had been repaired, but it had broken down again, and all the fresh provisions of *Hitachi Maru* were spoiled. So even that solace, that protection against scurvy, was denied him. Fate, which had protected him so marvellously for nearly ten months, now seemed bent on sending him to ruin. Most important, now that the decision had been made, was to move the coal of *Hitachi Maru* to *Wolf* and get under way with dispatch. So the crew of *Wolf* went on a twenty-four hour war watch in harbour, moving coal, while the ship's carpenters supervised the building of quarters for all the new prisoners in the Number Three hold of *Wolf*. That meant building bunks, closets, washbasins, latrines, and installing partitions to separate men and women, even as Dr. Hauswaldt and his medics struggled to clear the ships of vermin and do what they could to combat scurvy. The frustrating thing, from the doctor's point of view, was that he could do virtually nothing about scurvy. The men's hands swelled, they grew scabrous, their gums began to bleed, and teeth abscessed, and then dropped out. The only answer was fresh vegetables and fresh fruit, and *Wolf* had none of either.

The transfer of supplies and people from *Hatiachi Maru* to *Wolf* took three weeks, three long weeks, in which the radiomen reported daily on the search from South Africa and India for the

Japanese ship, and Nerger kept the seaplane aloft much of the time to make sure that he would not be surprised. The plane had a radius of ninety miles, which meant that he could expect six or seven hours notice if any British cruisers appeared during the daylight hours. Night time was a different problem altogether—and nights were more worrying by far than days. But no British cruisers or Japanese snoopers came to these deserted islands; Nerger's luck was really holding marvellously. The three weeks went by without incident.

On 5 November it was moving day. All the people who had been transshipped to *Hitachi Maru* came back; only Leutnant Rose and the prize crew remained aboard. Captain Nerger was almost ready to sail. One more day was spent taking care of last minute details. All the charts of *Hitachi Maru* were brought aboard *Wolf*, the navigation equipment, a big pump was torn out and sent to the raider to supply sea water for the Number Three hold, for washing down the place and bathing. *Wolf*'s officers went into the holds of the Japanese ship one more time to see if they had forgotten anything of vital importance, to bemoan once more the need for destroying so much of such value to the Fatherland.

Then on 7 November, the two ships weighed anchor, the mooring lines that held them together were cast off, and *Wolf* led the way out past the reef. A few miles offshore all the people—crew, prisoners, the women and children and civilians that Nerger called "passengers" lined the decks of the raider to see *Hitachi Maru* go down. Sixteen miles offshore, Leutnant Rose and the prize crew got into their boat and made for *Wolf*. A few minutes later came two muffled explosions, *Hitachi Maru* shuddered and began to settle by the bows. Twenty-five minutes later, the bow went down, the stern ascended in a grand arc, the propellers dripping as they rose, and she dived to the bottom of the sea. There was a little swirl of water, a few unrecognizable objects bobbed in the swell, and the seascape was empty. Blue sky, a few wispy clouds, hot sun, and endless miles of blue sea. *Wolf* was alone again, two thousand miles from the nearest neutral port, burdened with some four hundred prisoners, not long on coal and short of adequate supplies. There was plenty of food—in quantity—enough rice and canned crab and lobster to feed all eight hundred all the way back to Germany, but the scurvy cases were multiplying, and soon the efficiency of *Wolf* as a fighting ship would be in danger. These worries were on Captain Nerger's mind, as he turned *Wolf* south toward the Cape of Good Hope to run the first British blockade. Only one man stood on the poop looking backward as they moved toward the stormy cape: Captain Tominaga, lost in thought as he glued his eyes to the point where his command had gone down. And little Anita Cameron, darling of the officer's mess, scampered along the deck, quite unmindful of it all.

Wolf was making only eight knots now, the fruits of the divers' work dissipated in the warm waters of the central Indian Ocean where the barnacles grew big and fast. The hunt of the hunters was slow, but very thorough. *Chikuzen Maru* had reached her destination, and the captain, who had some difficulty in explaining himself in English,

155

got in touch with his own authorities. The word was passed to the British naval attache in Tokyo that something odd had been found in the Maldives, and a formal request was made that the British visit there and search for *Hitachi Maru*. It might well be that she had somehow been wrecked off these islands.

The Commander in Chief, East Indies, Sir Rosslyn Wemyss, was much too concerned with important affairs to pay too much attention to the Japanese demand, but in time a French cruiser, *D'Estrees*, did appear in Suvadiva Atoll to ask some questions. The French captain was a diplomatic and serious man, and he soon had all the information the people of the atoll had to offer. They told of the two ships, and the airplane that had flown around them. (Nobody had asked them about the airplane before.) They had the dates, about 1 October to 12 October, and they were sure that the ships were English. The captain of *D'Estrees* had no way of knowing what dispositions Sir Rosslyn made of his forces, so he came back to report on all this. Captain Nerger was very fortunate in the methodology of the East Asia command. Nobody had yet pinpointed him or come anywhere near it.

Three days out of the Cargados Carajos group, just before midnight, the lookouts reported a ship in sight. Nerger rushed to the bridge, first assuring himself that it could not be a British cruiser (too much smoke). His luck was holding again. Then he had an estimate of her course and speed from the watch officer, and began plotting his interception. He was at 21° S, 53° E, between Madagascar and Mauritius. When challenged a few hours later, the other ship raised the yellow and red striped flag of Spain, which sent Captain Nerger's spirits drooping, for Spain was a neutral and her vessels carrying Spanish goods to neutral ports must remain untouched. What a pity! It was difficult enough to find prizes, as Nerger knew only too well. It was just now even more essential than before that a prize be found immediately, for some of the soft India coal transshipped from *Wordsworth*, long ago, and never used because of its quality, had lived up to the bad name seamen gave it by catching fire, and here he was, thousands of miles from home, short of food, scurvy racing through the ship, threatened by typhus, with a coal fire in the hold.

However the strange ship at the same moment sent a message to reassure what its captain must have thought was an English auxiliary cruiser: "Spanish ship *Igotz Mendi* laden with seven thousand tons of coal for the British government."

Seven thousand tons! That amount would get *Wolf* safely home for sure. Nerger's spirits rose, and he set about his captain's work. Leutnant Rose went aboard the *Igotz Mendi* with his orders. No time was wasted in moving the Spanish crew to *Wolf*, but both ships got up maximum steam, and sped back for the quiet safety of the Cargados Carajos Islands, where Nerger could put out his coal fires, jettison the foul Indian coal into the lagoon, and replace it with hard coal. It took two days to get there; *Wolf* was limping noticeably now, even the seaplane had been so overworked that it had run out of most spare parts, and could not be trusted to do an observation mission except in time of crisis.

Nerger was very gentle with the Spanish officers of the captured ship. His grounds of capture were secure—*Igotz Mendi* was carrying a cargo to an enemy port, and was thus forfeit. But Nerger bore the ship and its officers no harm, quite to the contrary, the Spanish had proved friends in need. So a grand party was held aboard the *Wolf*, in the wardroom, with German and Spanish flags interlaced. The ladies were all asked to be present, and it was the gayest moment of the whole voyage, slowed a little, but only a little, by the total inability of the Spaniards to speak any language but their own. Indeed, that night the officers sang and drank with light hearts, and the lightest of all was Captain Nerger's, for *Igotz Mendi* had brought him another gift—a way to get rid of the women prisoners who were so much trouble to him.

The ships anchored, the work begun, Nerger lost no time in transferring the non-belligerents to *Igotz Mendi*, and the coaling continued. The famous Nerger luck was tested again on the second night, when the radio room reported very strong signals coming from a British cruiser, so strong that she must be coming very close. There was no point in trying to make a run for it, it was too late for that. Either they would remain concealed, blacked out, or they would be found and fight. Officers checked the ship to be sure no lights were showing, the guns were manned, and axes were laid alongside the mooring ropes, so if necessary *Wolf* could get under way very fast and make a fight for it in open water; steam was kept up in the raider's boilers. The Nerger luck held; the signals were very near that night, next morning they were faint and moving away. The ship was searching for *Hitachi Maru*, that much was clear; and had very nearly found her.

The captain faced a new problem as the coaling began. The second in command reported that if they were to take on enough coal from *Igotz Mendi* to make Hamburg, they must dump some of the copper and silk. Nerger studied the problem for a moment; all right, they would take *Igotz Mendi* with them as a collier, and replenish from her in the Atlantic. He and Leutnant Rose sat down and worked out a rendezvous schedule; the ships would sail separately for safety's sake, and would meet in the Atlantic. Pilots Fabeck and Stein now came to the captain with a suggestion. What was really wrong with their plane was its covering. The doped fabric had simply given up with old age, and the many flights had used up all replacements. But aboard *Wolf* was all this marvellous silk, light and strong, and the pilots believed they could make up a "dope" that would harden and stiffen the material to factory strength. There was nothing to be lost, if the pilots wanted to take the risk; *Wölfchen* was not going to fly any more the way she was, Fabeck said. So the fabric was ripped off, the silk treated and applied and treated again, and the two pilots got in and were hoisted over the side by the special derrick. The takeoff was fine, the plane soared up like a bird and circled over the mother ship, then headed off for a short hop, while Fabeck did a few cautious aerobatics to test the new covering. All was well. So Nerger sent the plane out on a scouting flight, to see if there was any further sign of the English cruiser—could she be lying in wait for them in one of the other atolls of the island group?

Fabeck took off again. Now up came a vicious squall, and when it was over, *Wölfchen* made her way back to the side of the ship. But she too had suffered, the new fabric was torn to ribbons on the wings and horizontal stabilizer; it was a wonder to those aboard that the pilots had been able to get home alive. That was the end of *Wölfchen*'s flight adventures. The plane was hoisted aboard, and the captain ordered it dismantled and stowed far down in the hold. It had been very useful, particularly in captures, and had flown sixty observation flights; its use as an appurtenance of a raider had been unique, and perhaps had accounted in part for the "luck" of Captain Nerger. Certainly *Wairuna* and *Matunga*, both carrying radios, had been impressed into silence by the coming of the airplane. Nerger and his pilots had shown what could be done with a plane at sea, even a little biplane as rickety and hard to manage as those World War I models.

During the cruise, Rose had been promoted to *Kapitän-Leutnant*, and now with his new rank he went aboard his command and prepared to live up to a very serious responsibility. The two ships got up steam and moved outside the lagoon. Then they parted, to make for the Cape of Good Hope separately, *Igotz Mendi* with a truly superior disguise that told almost truthfully what she was; *Wolf* masquerading again as a tender sheep that could do no one any harm, and looking the part more than ever, with her rust streaked hull and labouring eight knots. As they parted, Captain Nerger made the first rendezvous point—southwest of the Cape of Good Hope—definite. They would meet there and make sure that both ships had safely passed the British patrols.

Wolf steamed south, and ran into a southeasterly storm, not too bad a one, half a gale, and it was the first fresh cold wind the prisoners and crew had felt down inside the ship for all the months since they had left Australian waters in the winter. The scurvy cases were proving serious, but this cold seemed even to help them, and to keep the disease down a bit. Health and welfare of all on board improved almost immediately, and the spirits of the crew, as they rounded the cape without interference and for the first time in months felt near home, in Atlantic waters, began to rise to the point they had reached very early in the cruise. *Wolf* moved through the chill waters off the Cape, the heavy swell slapping at her, and the white caps spewing froth along her lower decks. The lookouts sighted a few smoke clouds, and the ship turned shyly away if she thought they might be cruisers, but tried to intercept them if Nerger believed they were merchantmen.

It was now December, the word was out in the Indian Ocean that a raider was at large, and all merchant captains were steering shy of strange ships. Captain Nerger did not have a chance; almost any tub could outrun him with his hull fouled with Balinese barnacles. He and *Wolf* and the crew had been a whole year at sea, an anniversary they celebrated on 30 November. It was impossible, any naval expert would tell you, but there it was. Nerger had taken a ship of the freighter class, one that needed frequent bottom cleaning, and adjustment of her sensitive engines,

161

and treated her like a sailing ship, and had got away with it. It was already an exploit that would go down in the annals of the sea as one of the most remarkable of all time, and Nerger felt far from finished.

The British hunt for him was now hot and heavy. On 2 December the cruiser *Venus* was dispatched to the Chagos archipelago. The *Juno* went to the Maldives to try to straighten out all the strange tales told by Japanese and Frenchmen, and her captain came back with the word that *Wolf* and her prize had most certainly lain in these waters for two weeks, the airplane scouting for them, but that they were long gone. Sir Rosslyn panicked, and put all his transports under escort the next week. That meant ships sailing between Colombo and Sydney, between Singapore and Bombay, between Hong Kong and Aden, all had to have some kind of escort, even though there was no German war vessel in the whole of Asiatic waters. Such was the furore that *Wolf* had aroused, so great was her power to cause the British to waste their war sustenance; she was worth an army in the field to the German high command, and here she was wallowing away in the very depths of the latitudes of the Atlantic, a dingy, greasy freighter.

12

Heading Home

Captain Nerger's whole attention was now turned to the problem of getting safely home with his ailing ship and his prisoners. He would gladly have put the prisoners ashore, the whole kit and caboodle of them, except that there was no way he could do so without sacrificing his major weapon—secrecy—and endangering his ship and crew. So the redoubtable Captain Meadows and the others continued as prisoners aboard *Wolf*, Meadows and his men having been aboard the raider almost as long as its German crew.

Meadows was still taking bets—that *Wolf* would never be able to run the British blockade around the Cape: that the raider would never make it up the Atlantic in face of the British patrols; but there was a hollow ring to his voice. He had certainly done his job well. One reason the authorities panicked in December was final acceptance of the Meadows bottle reports as accurate, and the sudden realization that Nerger had been operating under their noses for months and they knew virtually nothing of him.

Wolf was still seven thousand miles from home, even if she could steam directly there. It was doubtful, in Nerger's mind, if anything would be so simple. Off the cape, in very fine weather, he came upon a big sailing ship. After the usual hails and stopping, she proved to be the American bark *John H. Kirby*, carrying a load of Model T Ford cars, 270 of them in crates, which were destined for Port Elizabeth and Durban. It was possibly as well for all concerned that Nerger captured the ship, for the chronometer was off. Captain A. F. Blom did not know where he was, or that he was off the Cape of Good Hope; he had already missed Port Elizabeth, and he might have kept on sailing around the South Atlantic and the Antarctic Ocean forever if Nerger had not caught him. The cars were of no use. Nerger jokingly offered a new car to each of his officers, if he got it home himself. The officers appreciated the captain's little joke, as they liked any show of humanity from him, wrapped as he was so much of the time in his official, terrible mantle as captain of a German war vessel.

The procedure, once a ship was captured, was for the prize officer to send back a bill of lading as quickly as possible. Nerger would go over the bill and any other information about the ship, such as

164

coal load, spare parts, or anything important nautically. Then he would call the executive officer and have the bill of lading circulated among the officers, the stores officer, the mess officer, the gunnery officer and the engineer, just to see if there was anything aboard the prize that might be useful to some department of *Wolf*. Not since the first days had there been any looting of prizes by the crew; everything now was put to communal use, with the officers, of course, getting first pick of the soaps and toothbrushes of the captured ships. *John H. Kirby* had the usual personal stores aboard, but that was all that Nerger found useful. Captain Blom and his eighteen men came aboard *Wolf* to join the prisoners in the after compartment, and a hundred thousand pounds worth of automobiles went down into the deeps.

Wolf kept away from the African coast for two reasons, now. First was the fear of a British cruiser, but second was a fear of her own minefields off Cape Town and Cape Agulhas. The mines had cost the British five big ships, the *Matheran*, a 7,500 ton liner, the 11,000 ton liner *Tyndareus*, the 3,700 ton *Cilicia*, the 5,600 ton liner *City of Athens*, and the 3,200 ton *Bhamo*; and had thrown all of South Africa into a sweat. Here at the end of 1917 mines were drifting ashore occasionally, and the British minesweepers were still on patrol, trying to find the field, which they had not yet done.

Captain Nerger did not know the full extent of the damage he had caused, although he could suspect some of it in the nature of the "in clear" messages that had been intercepted over the last few months. Nor had he much time to consider such problems now, for the plight of *Wolf* was growing more serious every day. By December, three Japanese had died of scurvy and thirty others were in the sick bay, mostly crewmen. The prisoners took care of their own, as best they could, sleeping in such crowded quarters that the hammocks were slung three deep with other men actually having to sleep on the steel deck. There *was* a difference in the food of prisoners and men, the last few scraps of fresh foods were hoarded for the Germans. The prisoners had all the canned crab, lobster and rice they wanted; they brought their mess buckets up along the deck, filled them and carried them back to the afterholds, but they had not one single lime or lemon or orange that might have stopped the scurvy. One man in sick-bay went quite mad. His body swelled up enormously, his breath stank, and his teeth came loose. In his madness he pulled his teeth out with his fingers, and traced odd patterns in the dough of his flesh, and finally he died in agony.

The surgeon was on the bridge every day, making sure that Nerger knew how essential it was that they got home before the crew was unable to function. If only they could have stopped somewhere, and picked up some fresh food. But where! All the islands of any value in the Atlantic were claimed by the allies, or were so thoroughly patrolled and spied upon that for *Wolf* to stop, no matter how she masqueraded, would bring her to the attention of the British blockaders. South America was out of the question, many of the nations had declared for the allies, and American and British influence was so strong that any move of Nerger's would have been discovered. Even the

Dutch possessions, Guiana and the Dutch West Indies, were so heavily infiltrated with allied agents there was no hope.

So Nerger headed northwest, up the Atlantic, away from the African shore where the British cruisers lay, and up the ghost lane, where Count zu Dohna-Schlodien had patrolled so successfully in his forays against the enemy. Disease was on his mind, and so was the need for coal. The captain had laid his plans well; he had told Rose to meet him at Trinity Island, off the South American coast. For years that island had been deserted, and he presumed that it still was, hardly more than a collection of rocks sticking up above the surface of the sea. But in fact it was not deserted, but had been occupied by the Brazilians, who claimed it, largely on the instigation of the British, who had once been so close to Dohna-Schlodien that they might have trapped him here had they had the necessary information. Unknowing, Nerger set his course for Trinidad. But the fox was always wily. He had no intention of steaming up to the island and shouting out "*Igotz Mendi* where are you?" No, his arrangement with Rose was to meet him at a point a hundred miles south of the island, and then steam together, all being well, to the anchorage there and refuel.

Wolf headed northwest through the South Atlantic chop, the ship riding well as she always did, rolling in the swells but responding immediately, with not a single hesitation. The crews, sensing the surge homeward now, was in fine form; spirits were high and so was confidence in the captain who had brought them so far. Although Captain Nerger was not looking for prizes now, on the night of 15 December he came across a bark, three masted sailing ship under full head of sail, on his same general course (she was on tack, heading from France to Australia) and after following her all night long he stopped her. She was the 2,100 ton *Maréchal Davout*, with Captain Louis Bret in command, carrying a cargo of wheat. Nothing for Nerger but the fresh stores, and of course the new supply of prisoners that made life a little more difficult, twenty-seven of them in all. There was no nonsense about sharing out the fresh food with the prisoners. *Maréchal Davout* carried a good quantity of wine. Excellent, said the surgeon, as a preventative for scurvy. So the German sailors were now each issued a pannikin of wine every day, and there were a few more fruits and vegetables to be shared out.

Five more days of steady steaming northwest brought *Wolf* to the prearranged meeting place, and she waited there for *Igotz Mendi*. So complete were the plans of Nerger and Rose that it was only a matter of a few hours before the collier appeared, and the two ships steamed together toward the protected harbour of Trinity Island. Nerger's luck was with him—luck fortified by constant prudence. He had warned the radio operators to be on the lookout for any strange messages, and now up to the bridge came the radio officer, to warn that a radio station on Trinity Island was sending a message to Rio de Janeiro, in answer to a message addressed in the clear to Officer in Charge of Troops, Trinity Island. So there were troops on the island. Troops meant military organization and vigilance, and perhaps even British ships in the anchorage. Trinity Island was no place for *Wolf*, certainly. Nerger turned away.

It was probably his narrowest escape so far; British cruisers infested this area now, following the reports of *Möwe* and *Seeadler* and their forays in this region. When the message was intercepted, Nerger was just a few hours from the island, and by dawn would have been in the anchorage. Had that happened, an alert military, looking out its windows, could have had a message in the air in moments, and a cruiser would be dispatched. No matter what happened then, the hunt would be on at close quarters, with *Wolf* limping, yet forced to head homeward through enemies in the north who would know when and where she was coming. Brazilian Vice-Admiral Adelino Martinez now sent another message to the island: the military detachment there would be relieved the next day. That meant a government ship was on its way to Trinity, perhaps even a warship. Nerger abruptly turned the ship about, signalling *Igotz Mendi* to follow, and headed south, as fast as he could go to get away from the vicinity of Trinity.

Captain Nerger now faced the serious problem of coaling in mid-ocean. The swell was very bad, and even if the weather grew no worse he must wait. So he waited, moving slowly about until the weather abated and the ships could stand together, held by mooring lines, without either smashing their plates or pulling the lines and breaking them. The sickest of the prisoners aboard *Wolf* were got ready for movement to *Igotz Mendi*, for here they would part company. Christmas came, and with it for a few hours the gaiety of Christian countries, at least in the German

169

messes and aboard *Igotz*, which was carrying an excellent cellar of Spanish wines.

Then, a week went by, one might believe, while they waited for the weather to calm down? Not at all. On Christmas afternoon, after the big dinner, Captain Nerger told the officer of the watch to call the navigator, and ordered the ships brought together, sea or no sea. He was going to coal. No more time could be wasted.

The fenders were all brought out, huge complicated spinnings of rope which were supposed to keep the plates apart and prevent damage. *Igotz Mendi*, the smaller, lower ship, came up alongside *Wolf* and the lines were passed. Then the swell took over. A wave pushed *Igotz Mendi* high up its peak, until the deck was level with that of *Wolf*. Then *Igotz* dropped down, with a lurch, and smashed the side of the larger vessel with a blow that sent men reeling out of their hammocks, deafened by the clanging of the steel hulls. Another swell, another clang, inward in the prisoner's compartment. Another swell, *Igotz* came down at an angle this time, the coamings of *Wolf* caught her, amidships, raking the upperworks, and smashing in the starboard side of the bridge.

Aboard *Igotz Mendi*, the passengers were flung about like ninepins. Prisoners and passengers expected Nerger to back off with this evidence of damage and the power of the sea, but not so—he ordered the coaling to begin. It was a calculated risk, he knew there would be damage, but he also knew that time had very nearly run out for *Wolf*, and damage, short of sinking, was nothing as to that. The men went down into the holds, and sacked the coal from *Igotz Mendi*. But there was no gangway, there was no orderly carrying of the coal across and into the bunkers of the raider. The sacks were dumped into the cargo nets, hauled across by winch, and piled helter skelter on the main deck of *Wolf*. It was messy and filthy work, and the ship became black and sooty footprints trailed everywhere through her, in violation of all naval tradition. But the coaling continued through the night, the swell never abating, and by morning some five hundred tons had been piled on *Wolf*'s deck. That was enough to get her home.

13

Northward Ho!

On the morning of Boxing Day 1918, *Wolf* was a sight to arouse the pity of any seafaring man. Her rails were broken on the port bow, she was badly dented amidships, two plates were stove in the after curve above the propellers, and several other plates were cracked. Rivet heads stood out where they had been wrenched loose from their seating. The four hundred feet of her were covered with coal dust, even up to the funnel, the upper deck was slippery with the black stuff, scummy where water had reached it, and the acrid stench of coal hung in the air, defying the fresh breeze.

The chief engineer came to the bridge that morning to report gravely that not only had the plates cracked and broken in several places, causing leaks that were bound to grow larger in time, but there was no way of fixing them. The rivets had pulled out of the plates entirely in some places. Further, in Number Two hold, several couplings had broken and steam was escaping. If that was not enough, rivets had pulled loose in the engine room, the engines had been thrown out of line, and engine room pipes were leaking badly. The ship was taking water at the rate of eleven tons an hour, which put heavy pressure on the pumps. The two ships came together one more time with a grinding crash, as if to emphasize the engineer's gloomy findings, and then Captain Nerger ordered the rope fenders drawn up, and the lines cast off. He had enough coal to make the run through the blockade, it would be too dangerous to try to take more. Now they must try to repair the damages of the past twenty-four hours.

For four days the engineers and the firemen laboured to put the ship to rights. The carpenter took his crew down to mend the plates. They were braced and the rivets were driven home again with new mountings. Soft copper was driven into some of the holes, to stop the leakage. The pipes were wired up and repaired and covered with tape to make them sound. It was all emergency repair, and it was truly an emergency, for *Wolf* must be stuck back together again if she was to run the British blockade. In the thirteen months that *Wolf* had been at sea, the English had strengthened their blockade immeasurably, and Nerger was aware of it, although only in broad outline, piecing together the story from the messages his radiomen intercepted. He knew the war was going badly for Germany at sea.

The Germans had intensified their submarine campaign and with the building up of the convoy system had begun to operate in waters just off England's shores. The U-boats were concentrating in the English channel and the approaches to Liverpool. But just as Britain's sea lords concentrated their efforts in the channel, then Admiral Scheer launched an attack in Scandinavian waters. The new light cruiser *Emden* led a flotilla of destroyers out to split and attack the sea lanes, they raised Hob with the convoys, sank the destroyer *Partridge* and sent destroyer *Pellew* limping into Norway with her engine room full of water—and forced the British to assign a squadron from the battle fleet to the convoy routes.

The Germans were sinking around three hundred tons of shipping a day, well down from the previous year, but still enough to cause worry in Whitehall. Defences were being strengthened everywhere in the Irish Sea, with special attention being paid to Land's End. At the end of 1917, Admiral Jellicoe was relieved of command as First Sea Lord, and Nerger's old opponent, Sir Rosslyn Wemyss, was found to have muddled through and become First Sea Lord and Chief of Naval Staff. Considering Sir Rosslyn's barmy blindness to the existence of *Wolf* all those months in Asian waters, Nerger should have been cheered up, but he never made the mistake of underestimating the enemy and was prepared for a stiff run to get back home this winter.

Even as Captain Nerger made ready to run the English gauntlet, the sea lords were making decisions that would make it more difficult for him to do so. Admiral Beatty had now given up thought of a direct fleet confrontation with Scheer, for it was Beatty's considered opinion that the German battleship fleet was stronger than England's. So the effort now was to be to bottle up the Germans in their ports, and this meant trouble for any blockade runner.

For some weeks Nerger had been trying to decide what to do with *Igotz Mendi*. He could let her go, and send those women and other noncombatants off to Spain. But to do so would be to advertise his presence and his voyage just at the moment he wanted least publicity and least knowledge of his existence. So *Igotz Mendi* would come with him, and run the blockade too. The ladies and the others were blissfully ignorant of this change in Nerger's thinking, and kept waiting for the day that they would be diverted to a neutral port. The prisoners in the afterhold of *Wolf* now busied themselves writing letters home that they wanted taken by *Igotz Mendi*, and Nerger's officers dutifully censored and sealed them, all unknowing that it was futile.

On New Year's day, church services were held aboard *Wolf*, and Kapitänleutnant Schmehl gave the sermon, then finished up with a brief prayer: "God, help *Wolf* run the English blockade. Amen." And that was the end of Captain Meadows's odds on whether or not Nerger would decide to intern himself.

Wolf and her coal ship headed north, as the weather worsened. They could expect the weather to grow heavier constantly, for they were heading into the world's most unpredictable seas in the

176

most unpredictable season. Captain Nerger had hoped he might find better weather by heading up the middle of the Atlantic, but even in the tropics it was stormy that year, and though it was hot in the waters off the coast of Africa, there were heavy seas and nothing better was in sight. *Wolf*'s speed was down under eight knots now, and she was still leaking, in spite of the platemaking and rag-stuffing of Christmas week. She was moving north to run the blockade in January and February, the two worst months of the year, where ice and snow would be enemies every bit as dangerous as any British battle cruisers that might venture forth. The leaks grew worse, instead of better, and the chief engineer hied himself to the bridge to announce that they were taking more water than before, twenty tons instead of eleven. Furthermore, he said, he was not at all sure there was enough coal in the bunkers, even with the five hundred tons taken from *Igotz Mendi*, to see *Wolf* into a German port.

The crew realized Nerger's predicament, and they were very serious men, worried about their future, and about their ship. They would do everything possible to save both, but they were resigned to whatever fate held in store for them, and they were proud of what they had done for their Fatherland in the past year at sea. The measure of their luck was the shark's tail Captain Nerger had fastened to the bow, and every hour or two someone would make a trip up to hang over the side and see if it was still there. They headed north into the gathering greasy swell, and on 4 January, they sighted another sail.

"Clear for action," came the command, and men

went scurrying to their battle stations. Most of the crew ducked down below, so they would not disturb *Wolf*'s image of a dreary tramp steamer. Behind the false hinged plates the gunners were at their posts, ready. Captain Nerger ran up the red ensign of Britain, and overhauled the sailing ship, exchanging signals and lying like a trooper about his ship, his destination, and his cargo.

It was just as well that he had. The other ship was a Norwegian bark, *Store Brore*, two thousand tons, bound in ballast from Portuguese East Africa to Montevideo, a merchant of the sea, travelling aboard even in wartime, seeking cargoes and taking her chances. By all laws, of course, she was free from harm—she had no cargo aboard her, was bound for far waters that had nothing to do with the war, and was a neutral to begin with. Nerger steamed on, letting *Store Brore* go. But an hour later, his hunch told him that he had better take her, for she might let someone know about the black ship she had seen heading northward, and then the wily British would begin to put two and two together.

Nerger's hunch was confirmed when a seaman came to the bridge and asked for permission to speak to the captain. Such a departure from custom was surprising, but when the seaman came into the sea cabin, hat in hand, his news justified the breach. That ship, said the seaman, was the British ship *Alfon Alaw*. He knew because his ship had lain beside her port before the war, and he had come to know the crew very well. She had been sold to the Norwegians, perhaps? Perhaps, but just perhaps. Nerger put on all the steam he could make, and overhauled the bark again. This

178

time there was no Union Jack, but the German war flag flew, and the guns were unmasked. The ship stopped, and the prize crew headed swiftly toward their destination.

The Norwegian proved to be just what she said she was, owned by the Aktien Excelsior company of Oslo, but by then Nerger's disguise had been penetrated so thoroughly that he had no recourse but to sink her and take captain and crew as prisoners. He did, and the empty steel sailing ship went down to the bottom of the sea, as the explosions of the charges burst her sides. There was nothing aboard her of any value to *Wolf* except a few fresh provisions, very few at that because the hardy Norwegians subsisted largely on salt fish and salt pork. But there was a supply of potatoes, which helped with the scurvy cases, at least a little. That was all. The sinking had been almost futile, but Nerger had no recourse, once his suspicions were aroused. His duty to Emperor and country was to bring his ship back home.

The chief engineer was back on deck a good deal of the time these days. Now he came to complain that his condensers were breaking down, and that the ship must stop so he could make the necessary repairs, otherwise they would be lucky if they made five knots. And he had to have more coal. The damaged boilers were using more fuel to provide less power; that was the way it was. Captain Nerger pondered, and looked at the vile greasy swell that bedevilled him, and pondered again. The chief engineer looked over the side and spat. It was the devil on the one hand and the deep blue sea on the other; if they brought the ships together and coaled, they would suffer more damage, and what might happen to smaller *Igotz Mendi* nobody could know. If they did not bring them together, *Wolf* was going to run out of fuel and stop.

They were very near the equator on 10 January, when Captain Nerger decided he had to take the chance. He put a boat over the side, and sent it over to *Igotz Mendi* with very specific instructions for prize commander Rose. *Igotz Mendi* would get the coal ready in sacks, and her hatches would be opened and the men would be ready as they came up. So the ships were brought together, *Igotz Mendi* steaming up alongside *Wolf*, rolling in the swell. Aboard *Wolf* the deck hands rigged every possible piece of hemp as a fender, and lined the ship's sides with them, two deep. But the swell was tougher than rope—it smashed the ships together, moved the fenders and rubbed those plates till the sparks flew. The crash and lurch and crash of the hulls pounding kept men wincing and looking carefully at the plates.

Wolf's men outdid themselves in moving that coal on this day. Dirty and dishevelled, they grinned and sang and worked harder than ever. For as Nerger had told them, the coal meant home, and home was just around the corner. The coaling went on for twenty-four hours. At the end of it the lines were cast loose and *Igotz Mendi* staggered away, her starboard plates rubbed absolutely bare of paint where the ships had scraped so many times, her rails broken and dangling, her bridge so badly canted that it had a list of its own to port. *Wolf's* condition was even more perilous, for she was now making four times as much water as originally, her whole hull was strained, and the coal on her decks now covered the guns and made it impossible for her to fight if she were attacked by an Englishman.

So there were more desperate hours for the crew, to clear those decks, mend those plates, work those pumps and keep the ship afloat. Boats and davits on *Wolf* and *Igotz Mendi* had been bent and smashed. Both ships looked as though they had come through one of the terrible Atlantic storms of midwinter—and they had not yet reached the North Atlantic region where the storms lay. Now even the chief engineer said they had enough coal to make it home, no matter what. All that remained, a small problem, was to remain afloat. Captain Nerger set a course due north for the tip of Greenland. He was going to try again to pass through the Denmark Strait that separates Greenland and Iceland.

The weather grew steadily worse, as everyone now expected. *Wolf* was lucky to do seven knots, and she rolled and pitched in the gathering seas. She passed the Canaries, far out at sea, and the Azores. She crossed the Europe-America steamer lanes, saw nothing, and was unseen. Now came a new danger: the U-boats. The U-boat way had changed everything about the struggle at sea; U-boats sank on sight and worried later. *Wolf*, having been at sea for more than a year, had long ago been given up by the naval high command as lost in action, and so no one in the world (except the British) would be looking for her. To a U-boat commander she was just another very dirty tramp, streaming weed and fouled with barnacles, plates creaking and broken, that might best be sent to the bottom of the sea—even better if there was the

181

slightest thought that she might be carrying war material. By 1918 Germany had been driven off the seven seas, and a U-boat commander could assume that any ship he saw was an enemy of his government. It was rough on the Norwegians and the Swedes, but it was the fortune of war.

In 27 January, *Wolf* reached a point off the English channel, halfway out in the Atlantic between Land's End and the coast of Newfoundland. On the radio, *Wolf*'s radiomen picked up signals to the right and left of them from other ships, ships sinking and calling for help because they had been found by the U-boats. It was indeed, as the chief engineer was wont to say, a case of being between the devil and the deep blue sea.

14

The Blockade

They called it the great hurricane of 1918, and seamen on both sides of the Atlantic talked about it for the next ten years, sitting in dingy bars with their pipes, reminiscing as if they had been there. But the fact was that most who were there did not come back from this storm, for it was one of the most ferocious in maritime history.

On the evening before the Kaiser's birthday, which was 27 January, the glass began to drop alarmingly. For several days the ship's doctor had been making the men line up every morning for dousing with cold seawater brought in by the pumps and sprayed by the firehoses—just to acclimatize them to the change in temperature they would encounter as the ship moved toward Greenland. Now these precautions were no longer necessary; the wind blew, the spindrift reached the bridge, and any man on deck was doused automatically as the ship rose and fell with the surges of the waves. By midnight the wind had reached force 10 and was still rising. By dawn a hurricane was blowing in truth, Force 12, and the ship trembled as it surged into the heavy seas. Kapitänleutnant Schmehl, the old merchant officer, came stumbling up to the bridge, oilskins flapping. "If we don't founder I'll be surprised," he grunted. "I've not seen a night like this in thirty years at sea."

Rain or shine, Nerger had scheduled a celebration in honour of the Kaiser's birthday, with band concert and assembly on the poop for a patriotic speech. But when the time came, Nerger and the others were fighting for their lives and the life of their ship, and the Kaiser had to go unsung. The waves were sweeping up forty feet, to mast height, and smashing down on top of the ship's bridge. She rolled once, so desperately that Leutnant Witschetzky, on the bridge, thought she was really going over; then, ever so slowly, she pulled back from the brink, and did not capsize after all. The propeller was out of the water as much as in it; the ship ran in fits and starts, trembling all over as the blades came out and raced in the air; then caught in the sea; steadied; then raced again. On the peak, in the trough, and then wallowing; smashed by a huge wave; staggering; then rising back to the peak again. Witschetzky, who had the watch, could barely support himself on the bridge

184

by hanging for dear life onto a stanchion as the water surged over the metal.

The worst part was the very weight of the water on the poor, battered plates of the ship. Through Captain Nerger's immense energy and determination, all the coal from *Igotz Mendi* had been transshipped below, otherwise it would in the first hour have become a soggy mess that would never burn in any boiler short of hell fire itself.

The chief engineer made his way slowly up to the bridge, hanging on for dear life as each wave passed over. He had something to say to Captain Nerger. But even though Nerger bent his head close, he could not understand the man. The wind wrenched the words from the engineer's lips, and took them out to sea. Only when the two moved into the chart room and shut the door could he understand what the chief wanted. He would have to cut down their speed, said the engineer, there was too much vibration in the engines when the propellers surged out of the water and hung spinning in the air for half a minute or so. Already the vibration had loosened several parts of the shaft fittings. If they broke, then the power plant was finished, and so was the ship.

If he cut the revolutions, said Nerger grimly, then the ship would be unable to head into those vicious green seas, the sea would strike them broadside, and then they would most certainly be finished. The chief shrugged with the philosophical acceptance of his breed. He had made his report. The decision was up to the captain. He gathered himself, ducked deep into his oilskins, and hand over hand along the rail began to make his way below.

Hour on hour the storm grew worse. If Nerger had any hope that he would catch only the tail of the hurricane, he was disappointed, for they were in the middle of it, and the eye had not passed by yet. The cracked plates and loosened rivets now began to give serious trouble; the water poured through the crevices, and in the engine room, the fire room, and Number Two hold the water began to rise. The second in command was everywhere, constantly in tour of the ship to examine her ability to survive. He came below and ordered the two emergency pumps put into action. Almost immediately one of them broke down, and the engineers began working over it. Then the second pump broke down, clogged with the coal dust that lay under the water.

Eight hours into the storm, it seemed doubtful if *Wolf* could survive. The grey walls of water rose up above her and came smashing down with alarming regularity. The wind howled and sounded as though the devil were calling for their souls. Now making forty tons of water an hour, the ship was heavy and sluggish, and did not respond to her helm as she should. She began to hang over as she rolled—that was the water sloshing back to the overbalanced side, and with forty tons of it, more now that the pumps were down, all that was needed was a little change in tempo. All the sea had to do was bring up a right cross to follow the left hook, and *Wolf* would surely capsize.

On the bridge Nerger was the first to recognize the labouring response of *Wolf* as she rolled and hung up, and he sent an order throughout the ship, from the galley to the sickbay; every man was to go to his battle station. Kapitänleutnant

Schmehl then began organizing work parties, to go down into the engine room and help the black gang. The only hope was to clear out the bilges and tanks of coal and clinkers, and get the pumps back into action. Otherwise they were doomed. As the men assembled the water was up to the ankles of the firemen, and kept rising. If it reached the lips of the furnaces, and slopped in, then *Wolf* would expire in one long gush of smoke and smothered steam; without her engines she would go under in a minute. The men from the upper decks descended into the holds, to find the air hot and foetid with the stink of coal, and the water icy cold, so cold that they could only work in it for fifteen minutes at a time, and then had to come back up and be replaced by another gang. They had shovels and sacks and their hands. They groped for coal, they sacked it and sent it up the ladders and the companionways, and it was dumped over the side or on the deck, where it washed overboard in the next wave. Other men were building barriers of hammocks and sacking, trying to halt the inflow of the water from the injured Number Two hold. The chief engineer supervised the breaking down of the pumps, clearing them, and getting them ready to go again. They ran, and clogged, and stopped, and had to be torn apart again and cleaned.

The tenth hour came, and the storm was unabated. Two more hours passed, and the men were working in water up to their knees, saving the boiler room only by massive walls of hammocks and cloth that soaked up the water, and held it back from the hot tubes that would crack if the icy sea ever touched them; saving the fireroom with the same kind of dikes; the firemen were still working in water up to their ankles, but only their ankles. There was a good foot more of leeway before the end, before the fires would sputter and die in the splash of salt sea.

The thirteenth hour passed, with no change; the fourteenth hour, the same; the fifteenth, sixteenth, seventeenth, eighteenth—and the pumps caught and worked, and clogged, and the relays of men clanged down the ladders into the water, worked, shivered, and came back up for a bit of rest before going again, and still the ship rolled, and hung, and rolled and hung again, with no sign of any change in her action. At the eighteenth hour Nerger, on the bridge, felt a slight abatement of the wind, and a lessening of the power of the waves; then it began again. Somewhere not far from them, he knew, had passed the eye of the storm, and if they were close to the centre and it did not change direction, they must manage another eighteen hours of this travail if they were to live.

Then, as the slight lessening of the blackness indicated the coming of dawn—one could not say it was daylight in this storm—ever so slightly, Nerger could feel the change. The pumps began to work for longer intervals. The balkings Schmehl had laboured so hard to contrive were beginning to hold, some of the cracks in the hull were stuffed and not leaking, the water was not coming in so fast and it was going out faster; the weight and the inertia were changing for the better.

At the eighteenth hour the men were up to their waists in water as they cleared the hold; at the twenty-fourth they were back down to their knees and gaining; at the thirtieth, the pumps were working constantly, and even the most pessimistic old salt could tell that they were gaining. At the end of thirty-six hours, the storm was blowing itself out, the waves were down below the level of the deck—nothing more than a heavy sea— and the wind had stopped shrieking in Captain Nerger's ears.

Next morning dawned bright and very nearly calm, with no evidence on the horizon that the wind had ever blown, the rain ever pelted down, and walls of grey water smashed against the injured plates of *Wolf*. In the messrooms and around the scuttlebutt the men gave Nerger credit for saving the ship. Even the prisoners felt that the Captain had held her together that night with the strength of his own will and very little else. Why should mattressing and hammocks and rags save a ship? How could a battered leaky vessel, bottom fouled and trailing great strings of weed, her speed down by a third, taking water at forty tons an hour and her pumps broken—how could such a ship survive? It was beyond explanation, it took faith, and now the men had that kind of faith in Captain Nerger. They had always believed in him, now they knew he could take them through hell and back again—because he had just done so. It no longer mattered that his eye was cold and haughty, or that he dressed a man down like a country butcher working over his apprentice; it no longer concerned the men that his whole being was dedicated to his mission, and that all else was frippery and not worth caring for. These had become endearing traits, proofs that

Captain Nerger was something more than ordinary, and the officers and men had no fears.

The storm dispersed, *Wolf* steamed steadily northward, making almost seven knots. The air was calm, but growing colder; they were in the latitudes of northern Ireland at this point. It would be well to be careful, for this was the heart of the British defence zone, and the anti-submarine patrols were very strong. Nerger knew it, and the lookouts were doubled, and the watches cut in half in deference to the growing cold. It was all very well to torture men by keeping them out in a cold lookout's nest if you were so inclined, but if you wanted them to *watch* you had to keep them alert and fairly comfortable. Nerger would rather change lookouts on every bell than endanger his ship in the slightest.

The lookouts could not see much for the snow began falling, thick blankets of snow that came down for hours at a time and helped screen *Wolf*'s northward progress. On 3 February the snow fell all night, and in the morning when the watch changed, decks and hatches were buried under snowdrifts, and even the rigging had the softened look of a Christmas postcard. Captain Nerger was grateful for it, it was useful to him in avoiding the British, but it also made his task of finding the *Igotz Mendi* more difficult. On 4 February they approached the rendezvous point, south of Iceland and East of Cape Farewell, the southern tip of Greenland. Here they were entering the most dangerous of waters, not because the area was patrolled by the British so extensively, for it was not, but because the icebergs patrolled constantly, and the storms were fierce when they blew. If *Wolf*

190

encountered a severe blow it was not at all certain, except in the eyes of the crew, that he could take her through. Up above was the pack ice, almost certain to be thoroughly frozen over at this time of year.

When *Igotz Mendi* came in sight, Nerger and his men had a glimpse as in a mirror of what their ship must have shown to any who would see her. The Spanish ship's upper works were white, the cables and wires to the masts even were sheathed in ice. The decks were white, and icicles hung down from the bridge, and off the anchor chains like long spikes. The hull was crusted with ice where the moisture had condensed and frozen, and it rippled down to the waterline, where the friction and the sea water sloshed it off.

Nerger sent a boat to fetch Leutnant Rose, and the prize captain came over for a talk. They planned their separate efforts to break through the blockade; it would never do to try to go together, they would be immediately noticed by British eyes and certainly stopped. For the effort, Nerger detailed young Ensign Wulff to *Igotz Mendi* to give Rose a hand. Two petty officers and seven seamen went with him. After an hour, the boat took them all back to *Igotz Mendi* and returned. Nerger ordered it hoisted aboard, put the ship on war watch, and headed determinedly for the Denmark Strait and the blockade.

15

Breakthrough

At the time when *Wolf* had run the British blockade bound outward into the Atlantic Ocean, the
Royal Navy had a hefty force guarding various approaches. On the northern patrol line, the Tenth
Cruiser Squadron watched the Norwegian coast,
and one cruiser at all times was detailed to watch
the area around the Shetland Islands, between
latitude 62° and 65°. A year later, the force was
trebled, and six cruisers were assigned to this one
stretch of water, two on patrol at any given moment, night or day.

In the spring of 1917 the cruiser *Achilles* and
the auxiliary cruiser *Dundee* had spotted a fast
freighter, caught and stopped her and had her

identify herself as the *Rena*, a three thousand ton Norwegian. But Commander Selwyn M. Day, captain of the *Dundee*, was very suspicious of the ship, particularly because someone had painted the N of *Rena* backwards. He began looking around, saw that she had no visible wireless, that the wooden panelling of her passenger quarters had all been taken out, and that she was much bigger than the size Lloyd's Register gave her. So he went back to his ship and sent a boarding party, led by Lieutenant F. H. Lawson. The party made the strange ship, and went aboard. Then Commander Day noted that the stranger seemed to be tracking his ship. He responded by taking evasive action. All this had come in the middle of a grey afternoon, and Lieutenant Lawson went aboard the stranger just before 3.00 pm. An hour went by and nothing happened—no word from Lawson. Commander Day found the world looking curiouser and curiouser.

Then at twenty to four it happened: the Norwegian flag painted on the port quarter of the ship fell outboard with a crash that could be heard across the thousand yards of water between the ships, and the ugly snout of a torpedo tube thrust forth. Commander Day had been waiting, his men at action stations, the guns—two 4 inch—both ready to fire. Now, with this proof that he faced an armed enemy raider, he gave the order and the guns began firing rapidly. Just as the first and second shots got away, two torpedoes passed under the stern of the armed boarding steamer, not sixty feet away.

The ship was the old English steamer *Yarrowdale*, captured by *Möwe* and then outfitted to go raiding herself under Korvettenkapitän von Laffert. She had gone out to replace *Möwe*, which had returned from a successful cruise, and had got only this far before her disguise was penetrated. Commander Day turned across the stern of the other ship, and raked her repeatedly with both his guns. His gunners fired forty shells, which for the most part went home. Von Laffert tried to bring his guns to bear, but *Dundee* slid around and ran for the safety of *Achilles*, the big naval cruiser, and that ship's captain, F. M. Leake, ordered his men to begin firing on the unknown vessel.

For an hour the big English cruiser poured shot into the *Leopard*, for that was von Laffert's name for the new raider. For an hour the Germans fought back, firing their own guns, but one by one those guns went out of action, as fire spread throughout the ship. Then came a series of explosions, as *Achilles'* shells found the magazine and the torpedo stowage compartments. Finally, the bow grew red hot in the flames, rose up, and the whole ship, with von Laffert and his crew of nearly four hundred men, and the boarding party of Lieutenant Lawson all going down to a watery grave. The incident had been a magnificent example of German courage and nobility in the face of death, but it had also been an indication of the growing watchfulness of the Royal Navy and an increased success in dealing with the raiders. Since that time, with the closing in of the U-boats around the British Isles, English defences had grown even stronger. It would take all of Nerger's guile and his celebrated luck to get him through the blockade and home to Germany this time.

As Captain Nerger parted from Leutnant Rose, he gave one last order: Rose was to remain in this position for the next forty-eight hours, while *Wolf* ran the gauntlet, and then *Igotz Mendi* was to have her own try. Before beginning, Nerger made one alteration in plan. Rose had told him how on 24 January when *Igotz Mendi* passed two American transports, he had prepared, if either was an auxiliary cruiser, to sink the Spanish ship. His men had set time bombs on the bridge, prepared to fix the fuses at the last moment. While they waited, anxiously, to see if they would be challenged, Second Mate Susaeta of the Spanish crew rushed forward and threw the time bombs overboard, hoping that they would, indeed, be challenged. But they were not challenged at all; the two Americans were simply freighters going on their way. Rose was first astonished, and then angered by the actions of the Spanish mate, and he confined him to a compartment that was kept locked from that point on.

Hearing this story, Captain Nerger decided to take no chances with the neutrals and noncombatants, and even the sick, who were aboard his ship. He ordered every person who was not a member of the German crew to be taken aft and confined with the war prisoners, which then placed four hundred people in the two prison compartments below deck. They were to be closely guarded during the breakthrough attempt; he wanted no prisoner ruining his chances of survival.

Nerger now pointed the *Wolf* into the Denmark Strait, heading around Iceland, where he doubted that there would be a British cruiser. He would have trouble still, on the other side, as he sailed down the North Sea, but at least he would miss the heavy patrols he could expect just north of Scotland. His chance here was that the Gulf Stream passes between Iceland and Greenland and tends to warm the water enough to create a passage—sometimes.

They headed into the strait in a dense fog. The temperature of the air was 40°, that of the water less than 35° and the result was a pea soup through which no one could see bow from bridge. Then, suddenly, the fog lifted. Captain Nerger knew what that meant, and ordered a man to take the temperature of the water; it was down nearly to freezing point. Ahead of them lay a foggy substance shadily outlined above the water. It was the ice pack. They moved north along the edge of the pack, searching slowly for a channel. They did not find it. It was dangerous work, for darkness fell in midafternoon, and they moved in the gloom, small icebergs and floes all around them. From time to time a piece of ice would crash against the hull, grinding into slush, and the officers of *Wolf* would remember those weakened plates and loosened rivets.

A brisk wind blew up, and sent water over the bows; the water froze into icicles and sheets on the deck, and the men were sent out with fire axes to chop ice, lest the ship become top heavy and capsize. All that night the ship moved along the edge of the pack, seeking the channel she hoped to find. Nerger went down one promising lead after another, but they all turned blind, and he had to spin around, or back out; it was a dangerous business every moment, for as he toured one of these blind alleys, there was a very good chance that the grinding pack would close up behind him and he would be trapped, marooned with four hundred crewmen and four hundred prisoners in the Arctic winter. After two days of searching for the channel, Nerger had to give up. He was in too much danger and it increased every moment; he was burning up his precious coal supply; he was running the additional danger of delay, for if *Igotz Mendi* moved through and were taken, then his presence would be known or suspect. Reluctantly, Captain Nerger moved southward, back through the entrance to the strait, to round the southern coast of Iceland, then cross the North Sea.

As the ship began the run through the blockade, Leutnant von Oswald came to the bridge. He had some bad news to give the captain, said the prison officer. Nerger's eyebrows rose. It was Captain Tominaga, the Japanese skipper of *Hitachi Maru*. He was missing, and was presumed to have jumped overboard. He had left a note, apologizing for all the trouble he had caused; he had planned his move since the capture of his ship, because his bad judgment had caused the deaths of some thirty people. He had waited only so long because he wanted to make sure that the passengers and crew members would reach safety and now he felt they would. He hoped all his men reached Japan and lived happily in the future. It was a sad little footnote to the war, this feeling of personal responsibility by one single captain, and Nerger and his officers were much moved.

But here, near those dangerous Faroes, was no place for sentiment about a dead Japanese captain; there was Germany to be attained, and to reach it, he would have to pass through the lines of British cruisers and auxiliaries, and British submarines in the waters off the Skagerrak, then finally through the Allied mine fields laid on the approaches to the continent. As to the German minefields and the U-boats, he would have to take the risk. One of the officers suggested letting the High Command know they were coming, but Nerger sternly forbade any use of the radio. A single transmission could give them away to the British; they were better off taking their chances with the sea.

It was battle stations all the way. The men slept at their guns and torpedo tubes, and in the ammunition lockers. Off Iceland the weather was alarmingly clear, so free of snow and fog that they could see the glaciers in the distance. Bad news, this; Nerger wanted snow and heavy weather to get by the blockaders, instead of calm cold nights with the stars glittering beautifully in their blanket above.

10 February dawned bright and clear, and on the bridge Nerger stood with his binoculars, sweeping the horizon. It was the task of the watch officer, and he was doing the same, but the captain was taking no chances this close to home, in what was the most dangerous passage of his voyage. Then came the snow, and the heavy weather, and in the bleakness of it, *Wolf* ran the gauntlet and reached a point nearer safety, the Norwegian coast, on 14 February.

It would seem, and a year earlier it would have been true, that Captain Nerger was safe. But not in the early months of 1918. British warships had

been raiding the Belgian coast, and they had pun-
ished Ostend and Zeebrugge. They had laid mines
in the Bight, off Heligoland, and British submarines were very active off Denmark. Nerger no
longer had an up-to-date chart of the German
minefields, which he must presume to be changed
since he went out nearly fifteen months before.

On 15 February, *Wolf* moved around the Naze
at the southern edge of Norway, and then she was
in the Skagerrak, which was alive with U-boats,
E-boats, and British and German minefields.
Miraculously, she encountered nothing at all. For
four days Nerger had not left the bridge to eat,
and he had not slept a wink. But when the ship
passed the red buoy of Skagen, his shoulders
slumped, and he knew how tired he was. He had
made it into the Kattegat and the Baltic Sea, and
he was very nearly safe, if nothing new had developed in these waters. The captain made his
weary way to his cabin, sank down on his bunk
without removing even his cap, and in a moment
was fast asleep.

He was back on deck again on Sunday morning
to take the ship through the difficult Kattegat passage, and he did, passing so close along the Danish
coast that he could see the white houses with their
red roofs, the village of Frederica, the tall trees
around the squares; even the factories looked
beautiful to the men of *Wolf* as they came down
from the high seas into safety.

16

Home Again

In the safety of the Baltic Sea, Captain Nerger brought out the white flag of a German warship, and the great German Imperial flag with its red, white, and black cross and the German eagle. *Wolf* passed through the passage called the Little Belt, and in the evening came to really German waters, where the gunboat *Panther* and the mine-layer *Nautilus* lay at anchor.

"What ship?" came the challenge. *Panther* manned her guns and manoeuvred to keep in favourable position relative to the unknown grimy black tramp that had come charging into German waters, hoisting the German naval ensign, and behaving as if she owned the Baltic. "What ship?"

"*Seine Majistäts Schiff* Wolf," was the raider's reply. "Nerger in command."

"*Wolf? Wolf?* There is no *Wolf*," growled *Panther*. "Nerger? Nerger? Who are you?"

Nerger was impatient, yet cautious as always.

"Hoist the signal of the day," came the order from the guard ship.

No one aboard *Wolf* had the slightest idea what the signal of the day might be. After 451 days at sea, having travelled sixty-four thousand miles, it hardly seemed important—until this moment, when *Panther's* guns menaced.

"Nerger returning with the auxiliary cruiser *Wolf*," he repeated.

Then *Nautilus* broke into the message pattern.

"It really is *Wolf*," said *Nautilus*.

Still *Panther* did not believe it; but she unbent enough to send a boat, and when the spit and polish crew stepped aboard *Wolf's* seaworn deck, and saw the German uniforms, the German officers and Nerger himself, finally *Panther* believed them, and a joyous signal was sent to the fleet. At Kiel the word was greeted with astonishment, for Nerger and his ship had been written off months before as lost. *Wolf* was now cheered as she stopped and picked up the pilot who would take them through the home minefields. For the first time in fifteen months there were no lookouts in the bow or atop the mast.

Inside German waters, Nerger made his first report by radio since he had set out: "SMS *Wolf* has moored 17 February in the Aeroe Sound, mission accomplished. Ship full of goods. Condition of the crew. Thirty men sick with scurvy. Needing hospitalization, for scurvy, at least one hundred men.

202

Possible scurvy, most of the others. Please let us know what has become of our tender *Igotz Mendi*. Nerger."

Kiel had the wonderful news, and was digesting it now. In spite of attempts to harry the British and French at sea, the naval war was not going well at all, and the successful return of *Wolf* was something the government could crow about. That evening the papers had it: the Raider *Wolf* had returned. The first indications of what she had accomplished began to come out in the press. Germany was electrified because there was so little good news to report from any front. And when she put into Lübeck to discharge her cargo, and the authorities saw the silk, tea, copper and canned delicacies, that too became the public sensation of the hour.

There was one sad note, concerning *Igotz Mendi*. Leutnant Rose had sailed her down around Iceland, too, having failed to get through the Denmark Strait. He, too, had run the British blockade successfully, and had made the Skagerrak—only to run aground in a thick fog at the Skaw, the northern point of Jutland. This was Danish territory, and the Danes rescued the crew and passengers, many of whom claimed they were half frozen to death by the terrible trip in these cold climes. The Spanish mate, who had risked his life to throw the time bombs overboard, was let out of the lazarette just in time to escape what everyone thought was possible drowning. But the fact was that *Igotz Mendi* was safely stuck on a sandbar, and was rescued within a few days by Danish tugs.

The passengers were sent on their various ways.

Igotz Mendi was returned to her captain and her crew, and after a little refurbishment and some repairs, and a good deal of victual and liquid replenishment, she sailed off for Spain. The German prize crew, Leutnant Rose in command, was interned by the Danes for the remainder of the war, which in its own way was really a reward rather than a punishment, for Denmark still had butter and real coffee and sugar, and the Danes were not very hard on their German cousins.

All this word came to Nerger on 24 February, when he brought *Wolf* into port at Kiel. They came in in midafternoon, flags flying and the ship's band playing its frightful renditions of German patriotic songs, off key as usual. They steamed past the big grey hulls of the Imperial German Navy's capital ships, *Kounig*, *Kronprinz*, and the others of the famous Third Squadron. In the Wik, just before Kiel, they passed the Naval academy and the torpedo boats and submarines lined up there. As they passed, each ship honoured them with its men on deck, giving the salute. The guns boomed and the flags flew and dipped.

Wolf was now painted and scrubbed and decked out like a naval cadet in his best uniform, for she had lain at anchor off Flensburg for nearly a week while Kiel prepared all this pomp and ceremony for her. *Wölfchen*, which could not fly, was also scubbed up and tacked back together and brought onto the Number Three hatch as a showpiece, and brought happy tears to the eyes of the aviators in the crowd that lined the Yacht Club pier and the quays of the naval base.

Nerger moored and the ceremonies began. Iron Crosses were brought aboard by an admiral, and given to every man. Fresh rhubarb, ordered by the ship's doctor, came on and the men began to wolf it down, for the medico told them it was the best antidote he knew for scurvy. The men had new hats, which for the first time bore the insignia of SMS *Wolf*. The ships' bands of a dozen big war vessels vied with the tinny band of *Wolf* to make music. People cheered on the banks and docks, and the war rules were relaxed enough so that scores of small vessels bobbed in the water around *Wolf*. *Wolf* anchored in the place of honour, beside the Imperial Yacht *Hohenzollern*, right next to the black hull of another famous ship, *Möwe*.

Admiral Bachmann, the commander at Kiel, came aboard and offered his congratulations. Other officers came aboard and made arrangements for captain, officers, crew, and prisoners to leave the ship, all but the latter going into the best facilities the German government could give them.

In a few minutes, the crew began to disembark. In Kiel there was wine and beer and the finest food in the half-starved land of Germany. The crew went up to Berlin and paraded along Unter der Linden, Nerger in his full dress uniform leading, his officers behind him, all wearing their new Iron Crosses and behind them all the others, the nearly four hundred seamen who had made the trip with *Wolf*. They were surrounded by the finest troops of the Imperial Guard, and they were marched to the Palace, where Nerger received the medal *Pour Le Mérite*, the highest the Kaiser could bestow. The Kaiserin smiled on him, and the Crown Prince gravely shook his hand, and the people lined the streets of Berlin and cheered.

There was a week of glorious festivity, in which

nothing was too good for the men of *Wolf*. Dinner parties, theatre parties, the honour of all Germany was bestowed with lavish hands. But then it came to an end. The men of the naval high command, in their tailcoats and stiff white collars, decided what would now become of the officers and men of *Wolf*. Nerger wanted to go out again. But going out in the spring of 1918 was not in the German plans; the raiders had too much difficulty getting through, the war had changed so much that the submarine was the cheaper, more effective, and most deadly weapon. The high command could send out ten submarines with a crew of forty, where it took four hundred to man a big raider, and the results of the submarines were much more to the admirals' liking in this fourth year of the war, for the action had moved in around the British Isles, and a surface ship had little chance of success here. Besides, Berlin had the definite feeling that the element of surprise was now gone; the raiders had done their work and on the whole had done it well. But with the changing of the war, not so much material could be used for such peripheral activity. So, on sober consideration, the crew of *Wolf* was broken up, and men were sent to the fleet, or to the far north. The officers were scattered among the staff and the ships of the squadrons.

By mid-spring the passage through the Brandenburg Gate was forgotten. Captain Nerger was appointed Kapitän zur See, and detailed as officer in charge of armed trawlers in the North Sea. He fought the war to its end thus, trying to stem at sea the tide that was covering the land, and he never said a word about the comedown it represented to be at first captain of a sturdy fighting ship, plundering the enemy across the world, and then stuck in charge of futile little vessels whose victories were measured in terms of fishing boats and sheer survival. Nerger never complained, he never thought of complaining. He was an officer in His Majesty's Imperial Navy, and the *Wolf* episode had been a duty he had carried out just as he would have carried out any other.

Thus ended the cruise of the Raider *Wolf*. When the war was over, and the German naval rebellion died down, Nerger moved into the obscurity of a senior officer in a defeated and destroyed navy. *Wolf* was given to the French as reparations, and she went back to the South Seas, as the French liner *Antinous*, plying between New Caledonia and Tahiti and the old waters she had known so well around Australia and New Zealand. There were none to remark her there, for on the whole the Raider *Wolf* had been a shadow to the British on her long cruise, and when she slipped back into civil life there was no stir at all; only a few of the men who had been held captive on the ship for so many months ever bothered to discover what had happened to her.

As for the prisoners, they sweated out the war in prison camps and under internment of various forms. How they were treated seemed to depend entirely on whose hands they fell into. The radio operator of the *Wairuna* spent most of his time in hospitals, quite well treated. One of the captains' privileges, among the prisoners, was to be treated with naval courtesy, and this was generally granted to all the merchant marine prisoners, so they were well enough off. The civilians who had been captured were put to work in German industry, and one of them spent the last few months of the war driving what in the Asian euphemism is called a honey cart.

So the adventure ended in anti-climax. For in the defeat of Germany no one bothered to pay much attention to what Nerger and *Wolf* had done; they had steamed a distance equivalent to three times around the world, through the British fleet, playing hide and seek, laying half a dozen minefields, sinking three hundred thousand tons of enemy shipping, tying up millions of pounds of cargoes and hundreds of millions in the efforts of those who were trying to catch them; bringing back a cargo worth forty million marks to Germany, and finally, running home in through the blockade in a ship that would not even make six knots. Little *Wölfchen*, the first plane ever used in conjunction with a raider, had proved a new aspect of naval aviation. So *Wolf* was an historic ship, having done a grand and glorious job for her Empire, all in the line of duty.

Notes

The basic source for anything written about the Imperial German Navy's raider SMS *Wolf* must be Captain Karl August Nerger's own book, SMS *Wolf,* which was published in Berlin in 1918, before the war ended. Because it was a war book, it contains a good deal of German propaganda and long dissertations on the fiendishness of the British enemy; otherwise it is a factual account of the voyage.

The background for the story of the *Wolf* is laid very well in *Der Kreuzerkrieg 1914–18* by Hugo von Wäldeyer-Hartz, a German naval captain, published by Gerhard Stalling in 1931 in Oldenburg. This account of the German cruiser war at sea is based on German naval records and is as complete an account as is to be found of the larger picture of the sea war on the surface. The account of *Wolf*, however, is woefully short as compared to the stories of *Emden, Königsberg* and other cruisers, and of Admiral the Graf von Spee's cruiser squadron that fought at Coronel and then in the disastrous battle of the Falkland Islands that ended the squadron.

In 1929 Payot in Paris published *Le Navire Noir* by Korvettenkapitän F. Witschetzky, who had been gunnery officer on the *Wolf* during her astounding voyage. Witschetzky's book is based largely on Nerger's, it seems, as far as the facts are concerned. A gunnery officer could not possibly have seen the war through the same eyes as the captain, and Leutnant Witschetzky did not. His book has a considerable amount of presumably fabricated conversation among seamen, but is an interesting view, particularly of the prisoners and the forced passengers on *Wolf* whom Witschetzy seems to have got to know rather well.

In 1939, Yale University Press in New Haven published *The Cruise of the Raider Wolf* by Roy Alexander, who had been radio officer aboard the *Wairuna* on her fatal voyage, and who then spent the rest of the cruise of the raider as prisoner of war. Alexander's account is very interesting and useful from the point of view of the prisoners, and does not pretend to be anything else. So we have three good views of Nerger and his crew, one by himself, one by an officer, and one by a prisoner. Together, they give a good composite picture of the voyage and the adventures of these remarkable men, who spent so long at sea.

For the perspective of the Royal Navy and general allied operations during the war, I used *History of the Great War, Naval Operations* by Henry Newbolt (Julian Stafford Corbett in reality) an account based on official documents written by direction of the Historical Section of the Committee on Imperial Defence, and based on the official documents given the author by the Lords Commissioner of the Admiralty.

Volumes four and five of this work were particularly useful, one whole section being devoted to the German raiders from the British admiralty point of view. Newbolt tends to pass off the raiders as an anomaly much more talked about than effective, and probably this was true, except that the raiders did tie up huge numbers of British ships in strange and faraway places, ships that could very nicely have been used to blockade Germany and fight the very real submarine menace. The story of *Wolf* indicates how effective this harrying tactic was; its impact on people in Africa and Asia is quite lost in the official history.

The stories of other raiders come largely from my own works and my earlier researches, which produced *The Last Cruise of the Emden, Kreuzerkrieg,* the story of the German East Asia Cruiser Squadron, *The Elusive Seagull,* the story of the raider *Mowe, The Germans Who Never Lost,* the story of the cruiser Königsberg, and *Count von Luckner,* the story of the raider *Seeadler.*

Edwin P. Hoyt
Bat Mansion
Bomoseen
Vermont
USA

August 1973

The fascinating story behind
the greatest naval adventures of all time.
the saga of Horatio Hornblower

The

Hornblower
Companion

C.S. FORESTER

The complete and indispensable guide.
Fully illustrated with maps, charts, and drawings
by Samuel H. Bryant

P440   THE HORNBLOWER COMPANION $1.95

the adventures of
ALEXANDER
SHERIDAN

**Exciting front-line action in the mid-1800's
—starring one of the toughest professional
soldiers ever to bear arms for the Empire!**

by V. A. Stuart